BiU

C90 3977248

D1179256

C B

Six-Gun
Avengers

1866. In Randal, Grayson County, Montana, the court is in session. Most of the leading citizens are gathered in the courthouse, as it's the day Bill Serlich is being tried for the murder of his wife, Sarah, and her lover, Dan Beech.

Then a stranger checks in to stay a few days. He's smart, looks wealthy, reckons to be a preacher, and talks like a gentleman. For some, however, the stranger has all the hallmarks of a hired killer. Some report that the man is a ruthless criminal with a violent past.

Bill's father-in-law, Declan Rorke, owns most of the town and has paid big money to ensure a guilty verdict, but if the rumours about the stranger are true then he could be here to change all that: there's a score to settle.

Everything happening in Randal points to big trouble, and the stranger is there for his last vengeance – and he doesn't work alone. Someone else is heading to town…

By the same author

The Feud at Broken Man
Return to Blood Creek
Bad Name Drifter
Last Chance in Laredo
Hired Gun in Hell

Six-Gun Avengers

Frank Callan

A Black Horse Western

ROBERT HALE

© Frank Callan 2020
First published in Great Britain in 2020

ISBN 978-0-7198-3139-3

The Crowood Press
The Stable Block
Crowood Lane
Ramsbury
Marlborough
Wiltshire SN8 2HR

www.bhwesterns.com

Robert Hale is an imprint
of The Crowood Press

Typeset by
Simon and Sons ITES Services Pvt Ltd
Printed and bound in Great Britain by
4Bind Ltd, Stevenage, SG1 2XT

ONE

The man pushed into the courthouse was tall, but his body was stooped and his face bruised and flushed. His eyes were swollen and dried blood caked below his nose. Two burly men stood close, one cuffed to the prisoner. They shoved him to his place in the dock.

There were murmurs across the room. Some men shouted curses and some referred to hell as his destination. The women present sat together, close enough to see the accused man's bearded face and his clear blue eyes. His rich head of fair hair and the strong frame drew their attention. There was pity in their hearts for the man, but they said nothing.

In his dock, the man looked at the floor. His hands were still bound and his minders stood close. The cuffs were off him now. The minders watched his every move like cats would a rat. He was aware that so many people were watching him, all the time.

5

The legal professionals gathered and took their places. Papers were shuffled, whispers could just be heard, and men in suits shook hands, nodded and then moved to their places, ready to await proceedings. Jed Raines, attorney for the accused, went to speak to the man; the head of the supposed man of evil was lifted, so all present could clearly see the proof of a violent conflict on his face, reflecting the turmoil inside.

Raines said, 'You ready, Bill?' There was no spoken reply. The accused nodded and grunted. A clerk rapped his hands on wood, saying, 'The court will rise!'

The man coming in was Judge Henry Baker, a veteran of law work with thirty years behind him. He was square, comfortably weighty, and he sat down with a sense of his importance, before waving a pudgy hand for all present to sit.

The clerk spoke: 'Mr William Serlich, you stand accused of the murder of Mrs Sarah Serlich and of Mr Daniel Beech, on the second of August this year, 1866, at your home in Bannack, Montana. How do you plead? '

The prisoner was silent until a jab in his ribs prompted him to say, 'I did nothin' wrong, mister.'

'Then you plead not guilty?'

'I do.'

'Very well…we may proceed. Carry on.'

The trial began, with the court being told about that fateful day two weeks earlier when Bill Serlich came home from a trip out of town to find his wife, Sarah, in the arms of Beech. Soon all present were told about what happened by the prosecuting attorney, who glanced across the room before he spoke. He looked anxiously at a man with short-cropped grey hair and a solemn, emotionless face, who winked at him. The man was Declan Rorke, father-in-law of the accused.

The man of law for the prosecution was Frank Teller, and he spoke confidently. He was brusque, sharp and as formidable as his impeccable appearance, in a grey three-piece suit. He asked, 'On the second of August, eleven in the evening, you battered to death your wife, Sarah Serlich, and that followed your cold-blooded stabbing of a man who was present, by the name of Daniel Beech. My Lord, the prosecution states that Serlich is responsible for the deaths of these two young people. The woman was twenty years old and the man twenty-two.' He turned to look at the judge to say that, but turned back to the accused then: 'You were heartless and cruel, and you took the life of the woman you had vowed to love and cherish, along with the life of Mr Beech, who was the helpless victim of your homicidal rage.'

Bill Serlich said simply, 'Lies, Your Honour, lies.'

Heads turned to stare at him and some voices called out insults and abuse as he looked again at the floor. Declan Rorke shouted, 'We're here for justice.'

All heads fixed their gaze on Rorke. He employed most of the folk gathered there; when he shouted, men ran to obey his commands; when he wanted something done, it was done. On that day in the courthouse every slight movement of his hand or head made others look at him. His face betrayed nothing of what was going on in his mind or his heart, but folk were damned sure that he had a rage of revenge deep in him, and he was using all his self-control to hold it in.

In The Gold Bullet hotel across the street, the saloon had been filling up all morning. In the crowd were Harry and Gotty Wellman, the newspapermen, preparing for the biggest story since a bunch of drunken vaqueros had fired bullets into the general store and killed old Ben Hall and his son. The Wellman brothers were excited, explaining to each other what their angle would be on the killer over the way, facing the worst fate a man could imagine.

Then there was old Dandy Bell, who simmered with hatred and resentment whenever the name of Bill Serlich was spoken. He nursed his morning coffee and poured whisky into it, trying to drag his aching body into another day.

Sitting across the table, sharing his bad mood with Dandy, was Abel Marks, who was only too happy to share his thoughts. 'Damn no-good gambler, that man Serlich, and he has a soul that runs black with evil. I tell you, my friends, he seduced my

8

little girl, Anna, with his sweet-talk and promises, just a year back. Eighteen she was, and I snatched her away from him in the nick of time. Oh yeah, a man rotten to the core, that Serlich.'

'No need to tell me that, Abel. He done took so much from me at the card table that all I have left in the world is what you see before you now – these weeds, full of holes and worn thin like an old nag – that is the sum of old Dandy you see now. *He* done it. He brought me down to this. Bill Serlich is the spawn of the devil himself!'

Walking towards them, carrying a tin tray, with more coffee and whisky, was Kate de Giles. 'These are on me, do you hear, just because it's a special day for my friends! But I'm not sure about the man's guilt. I have to say that, boys!'

They told her she was sweet and womanly and Dandy tried to pinch her backside but she dodged wide and told him to behave.

'You think he ain't guilty? Kate, surely you can't hold to such views...' Abel said, but she cut in and stopped another rant.

'We don't know. It's hearsay, boys. Hearsay, not evidence. That man has always been polite and well mannered. He's a gentleman.'

There was a hard silence. They were stuck for words.

Kate was a woman who was now living her dream, running her own place and making folk happy. But it hadn't always been that way. She had pulled

9

herself out of the dark world of whoring in towns around most of Colorado, settled in Denver, and married a man of means whose money had lifted her out of the misery of such a life. He had passed to the next world when he fell off a cart, drunk as an end-of-trail cowpuncher, and he had left her a rich woman. So far, nobody had known about her past life. She prayed it would stay that way.

She was tallish, spare in the frame, and considered more appealingly feminine than merely pretty by the men around Randal, and more than a few of these fancied that the warm-hearted widow would make a fine partner in life. That didn't do any man any good at all. She wanted more and she wanted better. Yet she loved the place. She had no explanation for that. It was just a fact.

TWO

For days, Jack Hamer had been fretting about his charge, locked up in the roomiest of his three cells. The man was trouble, and that was the last thing Hamer needed right now. Early in the morning on the day before the trial, Hamer had been out for a ride, as that helped him think. He had taken a gentle gallop down towards the line of huts where the whores hung out, and past them, a few miles north, where there was nothing to hear but the hawks above in the grey sky, complaining about something.

Three years before he had come to Randal with more than dreams. He had had a wife and a son. Now they were wiped away by some disease that had ravaged the whole town and beyond. He had been left to cope alone. Then the world seemed to speed up. He was feeling like a wagon had left town and he was walking behind it, shouting for help, and not a soul listened to him.

The problem was with the daily struggle to maintain some kind of law and order. That was his job.

But with one deputy, it was tougher every day. Now here was this Serlich business, and the little town was big news. In the quiet time just after dawn, Hamer felt he could think straight, but all he could see was Rorke's face, hectoring and pressing him to take on the miners and the jumped-up politicians fighting for their scraps of power.

But this was such a fine country – he had come to love the Montana hills and rivers. He even loved the weather, which was sun one day and hail the next. Looking around, he saw the rich, lush land and the beautiful colours of the slopes and valleys, and he knew, deep inside, that this was worth fighting for. He turned his bay mare homewards, back through the whores' road and the bad side of town, where the no-good shiftless types rooted in for a while, stirring up trouble and boozing till they went crazy. The women were out, throwing old food into the road, letting out the dogs, and yelling insults at whoever was inside their hovels.

One day, Randal would be free of all this, he thought. *I'm making that my mission.* He looked around the place, as he did so often, pleased at the church and graveyard, smiling at the little schoolhouse, and the general store run by Rorke. Then a dark thought came over him. Wherever he looked there was something owned and run by Declan Rorke. They might as well call the place Rorketown.

Yet there was The Gold Bullet. At least Kate was clinging on to that. There was *The Clarion* too, and the Wellman brothers. They were on the edge, asking for big problems from Rorke and his bully boys. *Christ,* he thought, that's what I am... *a bully boy!* Only a year back he had been a free agent, resisting Rorke and his damned empire; now he was feeling a sense of drowning in the waves made by the Irishman's power plays. The man wanted everything. He would stop at nothing to have and hold every single thing in Randal. There were even rumours that he was involved in some robberies down on the Bozeman road.

He made it back to the jail with a heavy heart, but Ry Jodey cheered him up, as he always did. Ry, his deputy, was young and full of good humour. It could be infectious, but it could also be tedious. Today, the young man, short but stocky, with thick dark hair and plenty of evidence of his Crow blood in his skin and eyes, was spitting out coffee as Hamer walked in.

'Hey, you wasting the Lord's own produce?'

'Ah boss, it's like hoss-piss. Somehow I can't get the hang of cookin' stuff. We need a woman. Can't you employ a woman to do this sort o' work for us, boss?'

'There ain't no woman in the North West would tolerate me and you, my young partner... not one! We're like two mavericks, and we can't be roped in. Now I'll settle for breakfast over at the Nugget... but you go first. It's my turn. Serlich behaved himself?'

'Not a word. He's still asleep.'

'No, I am not. I can hear every word. I need coffee, Sheriff. Can you get Kate to send some over?'

Hamer looked at the man, who was now sitting up on the edge of his bed, with specks of straw on his blue shirt. Sheriff and deputy were behaving as though they had a condemned man in their keep, because that's what was going to happen soon, they were sure. Hamer thought the suggestion made sense.

'Ry, that's a fine notion. Git over there and come back with a jar of coffee, real hot and strong. Tell Kate it's on my account. Maybe some eggs?'

When Ry went out, Serlich shuffled over to the bars of his cell and put both hands on the bars. He looked across at Hamer.

'Sheriff, I known you some time now. I figure you are a man of sense.'

'I used to be. Randal rubbed it all out of me.'

'Sure. It's got its own hell. I been there. Truth is, I made it myself. Always been a fool. Should have been the kind of husband Rorke wanted for his girl… the kind that let the little hussy do as she liked. But you know one thing, Sheriff Hamer? I loved her.'

He let his head hang down and he stared into the sawdust. Hamer stayed at his desk, his feet up on top of it, and he thought about what the man had said. He had never really known Serlich, but he had admired something in him. He had never been a dog for Rorke to kick.

Now Hamer got up and walked across, just as Serlich lifted his head.

'Bill Serlich, did you kill her?'

'No. I swear to God, I did not.'

There were no more questions, as Hamer let the man be, as he went across his cell to wash his face and get dressed. Here was a man with most likely his last few days of life on earth ahead of him, and he was surely tired of telling the world he was innocent, but there was to be no peace. After Hamer walked across to fill in his record book, there was a knock on the door and someone shouted.

'Hey, Jack, it's Harry. Can I come in?'

Hamer told him to walk in, and he did, followed by Ry with the coffees and some eggs and ham on a tray.

Hamer and Ry sat down and tucked in, after Serlich had been given a cup of coffee. 'Kate says it's her best blend.' Ry said. 'The cook never spat in it, that's what she means. Usually, anything for prisoners is spat in or pissed in.'

'Don't write that in *The Clarion*, Harry,' Hamer said, with a smile. 'Anyways, I know why you're here. You want an interview with our prisoner. Go ahead while we eat. But keep it short.'

Serlich, drinking his coffee on the edge of the bed, stared across, and Harry Wellman took a chair and sat next to the bars.

'Hey mister… I could choke you real good, you sittin' by the bars an' all. You're takin' a big risk. I'm a dangerous killer, you said that two days back.'

'I'm sorry about that. The copy editor let his imagination run free, Mister Serlich.'

'Call me Bill. Write about me as Bill. Right? I suppose you're gonna say *Justice Pays the Bill* or similar? You like that sick jokey material?'

'No, I'm here because I can't write about the case and the trial really, can I? No, I want you to tell us about yourself. Where are you from?'

Serlich knew the papers would do no more than write something about how nasty he was, this killer of a woman. He said simply, 'I'm from the place where you say killers are from... hell, mister. I don't want to talk to you. I don't hold with newspapers. They're lie-sheets. Get him out of here, sheriff!'

The newspaperman turned with an appeal to Hamer, but the sheriff could see that Serlich was agitated, so he escorted Harry to the door. Serlich raised his voice, 'You're scum, all of you scribblers!'

It took a while for quiet to return to the jailhouse. Then, with coffee and food eaten, Hamer said, 'You want something to read? I have a book or two.'

'No, I want to git out and ride forever. I'm being tried by crooks!'

'Well mister, at least you ain't bein' tried by the miners' court. That would be no more than two questions and a lynching.'

Serlich didn't answer at first. He took in the information. But then he decided to needle the lawman a little. 'So, you're gonna make sure that true justice takes place, are you, Hamer? You gonna let the truth be spoken? Yeah? You tough enough to argue with Rorke?'

He didn't get an answer.

THREE

Hamer had seen Kate de Giles step off a stage when she first came. He had seen her stand and look around, lost but enchanted. From that first look, he had felt drawn to her. In between his pressures and chores, there was Kate, and though she had another man and she seemed to love him, Jack Hamer made it clear that he was there to serve the woman.

Every day he would call in to check that all was well. Kate liked the way he was polite, always raising his hat and calling her Miss de Giles at first, to make her feel good after she took that name and started running The Gold Bullet. She looked forward to his visits with a thrill of pleasure, and they always had a little chat. She called it her 'chin-wag with the law', and loved to tell folk how she had special protection if there was ever any trouble.

When Hamer sat in his office most times he thought of Kate, in between the working-day tasks. She would never know, but he kept a drawing of her in his desk drawer. It had been done while she sat and dealt the cards one night. Hamer was proud of his artistic skills, and he always thought that in another life he could have earned some dollars by his pen and brush.

In the early morning of that day of the Serlich trial, before any business was done and before the prisoner was escorted down the street, Hamer tried to laugh off his troubles by teasing Ry, and in turn Ry teased him. For Ry it was all fun about Kate.

'She ain't actually married, Jack. You could step in!'

'I know. You think I don't have that thought rattlin' around in my head most every day?'

'Well, do something about it, boss. Look at you. You just let things drift. I hope I ain't speakin' out of turn. I say this as a friend, but for God's sake tell the lady how you feel.'

'She's happy, Ry. If she's happy, then I am.'

'Nope. You plainly are *not* happy. You're like a mule being goaded to pull a ton weight.'

'Well, a man can like a women without botherin' her all the time with that romantic baloney. I mean, come on, look at me! I'm no catch.'

Ry had to chuckle at that, and then he said, 'Sure. You're a plain failure as a courtin' gentleman. I mean, when did you last wash your clothes, Jack?

'You suggestin' I have a stink about me?'

'Not a stink, exactly. What I'm saying is that you look like a woman's care is needed to bring you into the world of people. You know, that world outside this jailhouse, where folk sip drinks, play games, ride horses and such? Join the human race, boss, that's all I'm saying.'

There was no sense in telling the deputy what was really troubling him, so Hamer called for his prisoner to stir himself and got on with the jobs. Serlich, sitting up on the edge of the hard bed, rubbed his eyes and asked, 'When we goin' over there, boss?'

'Pretty soon.' Hamer said, handing the man some stewed half cold coffee.

Sheriff, can I say something now?'

'Sure. I'm here to listen.'

'I didn't do it. I didn't have any plan in my head to kill that wife of mine and the rat she was with. It was all a terrible tragedy. My Sarah… my beautiful Sarah…' He started to sob, and the coffee spilled on the floor. 'Don't boss, don't open that door!' Ry said, his voice carrying a deep sense of threat.

Hamer went back to his desk and forced himself to switch off, cut out the sound of the weeping.

Serlich had turned himself to the wall, standing in a corner, and he was beating on the wall with his fist, calling out his wife's name. Then he turned and spoke, through the watery tears and saliva covering his red face now. 'Sheriff Hamer, you have to believe me… we struggled, the gun went off. I never took no life in all my days. Sure, I worked too often away. I never spent enough time with her… do you understand that?'

Hamer nodded. He knew only too well that flaw in a man – neglect.

'I left her, and she was bored. Along comes this man with a smile and some soft words. You know, Hamer, I never could use the kinda words that lovers use. I was always too busy in my brain, schemes and plans, making it rich…I was blind to what was happening. You know, a man looks back and he sees all the mistakes, clear as a summer day… and that's what hurts like a stuck knife in the gut.'

He rapped the wall again.

Jack Hamer told him to go easy. 'I only got a flimsy wall… this ain't no prison. Desperate types have dug out of here. We have to watch these rogues like hawks.'

Serlich came to the bars and stared at Hamer, with his eyes wide open, appealing from his heart. 'Mr Hamer… am I one of them types? Them rogues?'

'You're a sure-fire pool o' piss in a clean room!' Ry put in, with a throaty laugh.

'No, Ry, shut it, will ya. Mr Serlich, if you ask my opinion, I don't see you as a rogue. You're not some bandit, some robber who left his scruples way back on the road. No, I think you are a man wronged, and you lost control. Every man knows what it is to lose control. Worse that that, you lost the woman you loved, mister. For that I feel for ya.'

The prisoner sat down now, squatted on the dirty floor. He spoke quietly. 'I appreciate that Mr Hamer. But still, as you're offerin' opinions, what are my chances of avoiding the hangman?'

Hamer thought for a while, his mind churning over all the things that Declan Rorke had been busy with, making sure that his enemy would swing. He decided that a sweet, wanted lie was better than a hard fact. 'Mr Serlich, I think you have a sportin' chance of walking back to my jail and then gatherin' your belongings to go home.'

Ry gave a wheezing noise, and then a sigh. The prisoner tried to look cheered. But they all knew it was a sweet lie.

'Ten minutes boss, then we have to move out.' Ry said.

Hamer told the prisoner to dress and smarten up. 'Get a shave, mister. Wash. Wear this...' He threw a clean shirt through the now open cell-door. Ry watched, rifle pointed at Serlich. 'I keep a clean shirt ready. The jury like a smart accused man.' Hamer said this, trying to sound convincing. *This* jury would not be swayed by a suit of the best material in New York.

Serlich did his best. The facilities were basic. But Hamer had left a clean flannel and a bowl of clean water. He even allowed a razor. The man was not going to cut his throat, and even if he did, it would be a better way out of life than in a noose.

The three men walked steadily and purposefully down the street, Ry behind the prisoner, pointing his rifle at the man's back, Hamer only pausing to wave at Kate, who was at her window.

FOUR

The Gold Bullet was red brick, with seven rooms for guests and a downstairs saloon. There were two tall chimneys, an attic window and a shaky balcony with a wooden palisade along it; a small veranda at the front had wood to match the upper balcony, and broad but worn front steps led up to a strong wooden door. It needed some repairs and a lick of paint maybe, but Kate de Giles loved it. She had grown to feel a part of it, and the place was deep in her heart.

She loved that the locals knew her affectionately as Blue-eyed Kate. Her blood was from the north of the old continent, up in Norway, and she looked the part: blonde and blue-eyed, and with muscles made by hard work. Sitting around in drawing-rooms and wearing flowery gowns had never been her life.

On this day she had spent some time before the drinkers arrived thinking about Bill Serlich. Once they had kissed. It had been at a shindig for some friend of Rorke's, and Bill had indulged in strong beer too much, the same as she had with brandy, and there had been a short embrace. But she recalled the look he had given her with a stab of excitement in her breast. His look had said he wanted her. But he was a gentlemen. He had apologised and even given a little nod of his head, as he blamed the drink for his bad manners.

Well, she remembered the bad manners and they were not a bad memory. But the day was going to be busy and she was soon making ready, along with her staff, for the rush of the crowd. They expected the day to bring a death verdict, and then, maybe in a few days, there would be a man having his neck stretched along the road a-ways.

'Bill Serlich has had it coming for two years or more, and he's gonna have his neck stretched, you'll see!'

This was Watt Wright, an old-timer who spent all the daylight hours in the corner of The Gold Bullet, bumming drinks and telling tall stories. Nobody listened to him these days. They just laughed. But he rapped out those words as he jutted his raddled face forwards towards his old partner Red Simon, and said, 'Ten bucks says I'm right.'

'You ain't got ten bucks!' Red laughed.

'Fine… well, I'll lay my boots agin your ten dollars. These boots is worth twenty. They cost me thirty.'

The Wellman brothers, settled comfortably by a long table that had heaps of notes and files on it, sat back and took a rest from their scribbling and enjoyed the entertainment provided by Watt and Red, who generally kept the customers amused in Kate de Giles' hotel and bar.

Dandy Bell shuffled across to the front of the hotel, where he could look through a window, and out across to the courthouse. Watt Wright was thinking about using the spittoon, but then, as Kate walked by, he changed his mind and went on chewing some tobacco. He called across to Dandy, 'Hey, as one old-timer to another, what's goin' on now?'

'Not a thing. Silent as the tomb. But I guess there's plenty of movement in Serlich's chest. His damned evil heart will be thumping a hundred to the minute, I tell ya.'

It was Gotty Wellman who decided that something had to be done. He had told his little brother that a story like this had to have some whipping up. He stood up, looked around and saw that there was a lull in the talk. It was just the opportunity to boost that palpable sense of expectancy he sensed. 'Look, you good folk of the best mining town in Montana territory, this is a momentous day. Why? Because this is a day when Lady Justice does what she is supposed to do. By that I mean kick a rogue down, drag him along the dirt and string him up! Now as my brother and I run the press around here, we're gonna liven things up and mark this day. Oh yes, there will be fifty dollars coming to the man who brings Serlich's boots to the Clarion's office. Fifty dollars!'

'What do you want the boots for?' Dandy shouted.

'You'll see when you read the paper this week, old friend!'

There was general laughter. Gotty went on, regardless: 'Now you all know us. You know that Harry here was born Heinrich, and I am really Gottfried. We are Germans in the blood, of course. But we tell you this – that we are Americans and Montanans, and our purpose in telling the world about what happens here today is that we're leading the states in carrying out pure and manly justice. We tolerate no weakness here in Randal, right?'

They all cheered. But Kate was now ready to stop the excitement. She said, 'Gotty, that's quite enough. We all know you're dipping your toes in politics and I won't have The Gold Bullet sullied by the rants of the hustings, do you hear?'

Gotty and Harry mumbled some kind of apology. Glasses were refilled. The barmen were busier than ever as the clock ticked on, and they all imagined what was happening to the accused across the street.

Dandy Bell paced up and down, sighing and complaining, mostly to himself. Finally he went into a rant, addressing everybody present. 'You know, this town has gone to the dogs When I first came here, thinkin' of how rich I was meant to be, with gold just seeping out of the rock and trickling down the rivers, I never thought that this could be the sort of place that folk went around with guns and shot their womenfolk. Never thought the day would come! Here's this man, among us decent folk, and he shoots his wife!'

'Now, Dandy, this is hearsay,' Kate said, going to him and taking his arm, meaning to lead him towards a chair where he could have a few drinks and maybe sleep. 'We don't know the truth. No, that's for a court of law to decide. Would you accept that?

'Well naturally, but he's guilty as hell. It's written on his face. He's evil, come amongst decent people. The law will be applied with a sure hand.'

Abel Marks now joined in, as he recovered slightly from the effects of too much strong drink: 'Yep, a sure hand... no soft law round these parts!'

'You mean like last year, when the miners decided that the man mixed up with some robbers was strung up? He never had a fair hearing!' Kate said. She ordered a whisky for Dandy.

The clock was ticking on, and the day was warming up. Folk started wiping their faces with bandanas and asking for water. A card game started in one corner, and Gotty Wellman was writing up some notes. There was a lull and a few minutes of silence. But then the doors swung open and in walked a tall man, smart and hated, carrying a light bag; he was swarthy, with fine features and of light build. His boots jangled with spurs and over

27

one shoulder he carried a rifle in a saddle-case. Every head in the room turned to look at him as he stepped slowly towards the reception at the end of the bar counter.

There was quiet, so that everyone heard him say, 'James Kamer, checking in. Two nights maybe.' He waited for the barman to grab a book and write something down. The stranger didn't look around. He just fixed his gaze on the barman's face and waited.

'You're lucky we have a room, mister. It's a busy day for Randal.'

'Oh yeah? You got a band or some actors in town maybe?'

'No, sir. We have a trial. You not heard of the Rorke murder?'

'I don't read much, and I don't listen to gossip.'

He was given a sheet of paper to fill in, and then he handed over some dollars.

The barman looked him up and down. 'You got any more bags… in the stables maybe?'

'No more bags. Show me the room, and then I'll come down to eat.'

Kate now walked across, reached out to shake the man's hand and said, 'Welcome to Randal, sir. I can have you some food real soon. You come down when you're ready.'

The stranger smiled at her, and he gave a little nod of the head. 'Why thanks, ma'am. That's real good of you.' He lifted his hat.

Kate was impressed, but the mood was spoiled by Dandy, who yelled out, 'You picked a good day to come, mister. We're gonna hang a killer!'

The stranger looked across at the old-timer, but his face showed no response. As he walked up the stairs, all eyes were on him. The barman whispered to Kate, 'He's called James Kamer... from Nebraska.'

Kate liked the look of him, and she liked the thought of a new face around the place.

'I think I seen the man before,' Gotty Wellman said. 'Can't say where... but his face is familiar!'

There was the sound of a commotion across the street and everyone scrambled across to the door and the windows. There was deputy Ry Jodey, running out and heading towards the jailhouse, as if there was something important going on.

'Follow him, Harry!' Gotty said, pushing his brother towards the door. 'Follow him!'

Harry rushed out, notebook in his hand.

'Reckon there's some evidence they need,' Dandy put in.

'They don't need evidence!' Another man said, 'The man's neck is to be stretched, or I'm a bull moose!'

A creak on the staircase made all heads turn, and there was the stranger, smart now, with a black vest and his long hair combed neat. His long-sleeved shirt was fastened at the cuff, and his trousers looked pressed. He had no smile on his face. He just moved real steady and sure. Abel Marks took one look, and whispered to Dandy, 'He moves like a gunslinger… I seen that walk afore. We'll have to watch this son of a puma! He's the sort to bide his time and then pounce. He's here for a reason, my friend.'

Kate had a gentleman on her hands, and that was welcome news. If her man, Cal Delano, wasn't due home soon, she would maybe have been keen to spend some time with the guest. In fact, she would still do that. He was too tempting to resist, and it was business, after all. Her three young dancers up in their rooms, making ready for the evening's shows, were going to enjoy having such a smart man around, too.

When the man reached floor level and came to Kate with his arm outstretched, she felt herself warm to him even more.

'Lead me to some dinner, ma'am… and won't you join me?'

Kate accepted and walked with him. 'I'm Kate de Giles, by the way; I run the place, Mr Kamer. Good to have a gentleman in Randal.'

'Too few of us left, Kate, too few.' Now he laughed a little and pulled back a chair for her to sit on, making her comfortable before sitting down himself.

The table was set, and with a bottle of wine. He filled two glasses. Then, as they raised their glasses, he said, 'Here's to an old friend of mine, Declan Rorke…he'll be so pleased to see me!'

'He doesn't expect you, then, Mr Kamer?' Kate asked.

'Oh no, not at all. In fact, it will be a shock.' He laughed again and then touched his glass on hers. They drank again.

The entire room heard the man say he knew Rorke, and suddenly, he wasn't welcome.

FIVE

Frank Teller was warming to his task in court now, and after explaining to the court that Bill Serlich was a chancer who had always made enemies, he set about his questioning.

'Mr Serlich, would you say that you loved your wife, Sarah?'

'Of course. I married her. We were in love. I had never had a woman like that in my life before. Her death wrecked me, to be honest. It was a horrible accident...I've never fired a gun since, not of any description.'

'An accident? You are telling this court that your wife was *accidentally* killed that fateful night?'

'Yes, sir. I came home, and I'd taken a few drinks. I was tired after a long journey and I stopped off for a few drinks. Would to God that I never did! She might be alive now.'

He paused, and with a hand to his forehead, he dipped his head down to hide his feelings. Teller let him have half a minute.

'Let's get the facts right, Mr Serlich. Take us through the events of that night.'

Serlich gathered his composure again. 'Fine. Well, I'd been down to Bozeman. It was very late. After the drinks I came home and there they were, Beech sitting on the bed and my wife, only half... half dressed, in the middle of the room, trying to dress, and in a hurry to do so. I started yelling and walked towards Beech, who stood up and took his gun from its holster, hung over the bed-end. As he reached for it, I shot once and his gun fell to the floor... I was aiming at his leg. But Sarah, she jumped at me... she jumped at me and tried to take the gun. That's how it all happened, sir. She tugged at that revolver and it swung around to her chest. Somehow, a bullet hit her in the heart. There was no chance of saving her, sir. That's what happened.'

The court was entranced by all this, and when he stopped talking there were murmurs. Some were calling him a liar, and some made sounds which seemed to be sympathetic towards Serlich.

'But Mr Serlich, Daniel Beech died too. It seems fortunate for you that he did. You meant to wound him only, and he died. If he had only been wounded, he could easily have shot you, probably fatally, as you wrestled with the gun and with your wife's grip on it.'

Serlich looked around for a minute, as if appealing for common sense. 'If you put it that way, then yes, it was lucky for me. But I never meant to kill either of them. I am no murderer, Mr Teller.' He turned to Judge Baker, with a silent appeal for his understanding. He remained impassive and merely frowned.

'Mr Serlich, you put to this court the view that a strange and unlikely series of events led to these two deaths, while you yourself were unscathed. Seems a little far-fetched, don't you think, that you should survive? Do you think you have a guardian angel?'

There were some laughs in court. But Judge Baker stared at the culprits, threateningly.

'It's the truth. I spoke the truth. There were no witnesses…'

Teller made a sarcastic sneer, 'Oh yes, very convenient! I suggest, Mr Serlich, that on that night in question, you went to your home, drunk and moody, and when you saw those two people, as you expected to do, you coldly shot both of them dead.'

'No!' Serlich snapped out. 'No! That was not it at all! I was mad at Beech, of course. I did pull a gun and intend to wound him.'

Teller rapped a hand on the table by his side, so that the sound would catch the attention of the whole court. Then he broke the uneasy silence with a piercing question: 'You are asking this court to believe that you, a man overcome with a passionate jealousy, took the time to think that you would merely wound the man?'

'Yes. That's exactly what I'm saying.'

'Then you take us all for fools, Mr Serlich! The truth is very different from your account. Mr

Serlich, would you agree that you have a certain reputation around these parts… a reputation as, if I may put it boldly, as a Lothario?'

'A Lothario? You're a comedian, Mr Teller, you want to spin crazy yarns and tall tales!'

Teller did not like that reply at all. He pressed the point. 'There is ample evidence, Mr Serlich, that you have had affairs of the heart with at least three young women of this town. I can bring witnesses to the stand to prove it. You are what may politely be termed a "heart-breaker". What I suggest to this court is that you could not bear the thought that you were being cuckolded, and that Mr Beech was the object of your terrible wrath that night. He had to die, didn't he, Mr Serlich… *he had to die*!' Teller spoke the last words after moving towards Serlich, snapping them out with a strength and a passion that made most of the court sit back in shock.

'This is all in your mind, Sir,' Serlich replied. 'I loved Sarah, and if I had time with other women before that, well, that was before I married. I never was unfaithful to Sarah. That is the truth… I swore on the Holy Book today, and I honour that swearing.' He looked around at the faces of the jury as he said the last words.

'No more questions at the moment, Your Honour,' Teller said, and returned to his seat.

Judge Baker ordered a break for drinks and air. The heat was building.

In the jury room, the men all milled around and waited for some comment from the man elected as leader, who was Declan Rorke's cousin, though the Judge had no knowledge of that. 'It's a clean case, my friends. The man is a liar and he's guilty. Nothing will change that, will it?' He took a fat roll of notes from his pocket and passed around a bundle of dollars to each man present. 'See, Mr Rorke is rewarding us all for making sure that a guilty man gets what he deserves. Enjoy spending this, gentlemen!'

Hands were held to take the cash, one after the other, as the man walked around the table. All, that is, except for one. There was a young man among them who stared at the money and then put both his hands in his pockets.

'Take the dollars, boy!' The man said.

'No. I believe in the law and in a fair trial. I shall report what you are doing to Judge Baker.'

'Judge Baker has received ten times this amount, son! Don't be a fool… take the dollars and shut your mouth.'

The young man walked out, saying, 'No. I shall stand back from such iniquity!' He took a walk at the back of the courthouse, with Hamer keeping a close watch on him.

The jury members all enjoyed a laugh at what they had just witnessed. Rorke's cousin chuckled so that his double chins wobbled, and one of the oldest jury members said, 'He'll toe the line, one way or another. He's new here. Baker thought he would be sound.'

In a back room, which was set up as a temporary bar, Declan Rorke and his lawyer, Teller, went through the next stage. Rorke, squat and wide, filling his chair comfortably and spreading his legs across the wooden floor, said, 'They seem to be taking some pity on him, Frank. When he spoke about my Sarah, it came across as, well... genuine. That's because he's a skilled liar, and he can apply some charm.'

Teller downed the third whisky of the day. 'Declan, listen to me. Jed Raines is going to ask for a lot more sympathy now, but it will all be wasted time. We know the damned verdict!'

'Sure. I remember well the first time my Sarah walked out with the man. They all whispered that he was no good. I heard the talk. I tried hard to keep it from her. I tried to get him out of town as well, but it didn't work...'

'You mean you couldn't buy Serlich – like you buy everybody else?' He smiled, and filled his glass again.

Serlich and Jed Raines, attorney for the accused, spoke while Sheriff Hamer and Ry stood by, with Ry cuffed to the prisoner. Raines could only say, 'Tell them about Sarah, Bill. Show them how you loved her. Right?'

There was despair in Serlich. He knew that there was no chance for him. Breaking out was the only option. He looked around every minute to see if there was a split second open to an escape attempt. But he was closely watched. Young Ry Jodey kept a rifle barrel to Serlich's cheek.

'Listen, Bill, though we know what Rorke can do, our best chance is to get the public on your side… get them to see what happened, and any sentence as a very wrong, morally wrong thing. You see?'

'I see, but it ain't any use. They want me to swing.'

'Whatever the case, we fight on.' Raines walked around, his mind working hard, weighing up every angle of argument.

Then they were all in place again, and Bill Serlich, beginning to accept his fate, was losing the will to fight. He had no idea that a young man sitting in the jury was on his side, and was starting to consider something that might work along with the true law of the land. The young man stared at the judge, and felt sick at the thought of his twisted soul, that he would be bribed.

'Your Honour,' Raines began, 'I call Declan Rorke.'

Rorke walked out, sat still and firm, waiting for the questions. Every move his body made caused a ripple of interest in court. He took the oath, his broad hand on the Bible.

'Mr Rorke, I would like you to describe the nature of Sarah and Bill Serlich's friendship, when they first met.'

'At first it was good. I had no idea he was a snake, a selfish hog, at that time.'

Raines complained to Judge Baker at this, and the Judge pretended to reprimand Rorke, who chuckled at the playing around they indulged in. But he answered. 'Mr Raines, at first he fooled everyone. Oh yes, he lies so well. It's plain to see... he wanted my money! Oh yes, what a catch Sarah was! He looked at her and he saw dollars... lots of them. Every fraudster this side of Kansas wants to find a rich daughter and land to inherit. This man saw that he had my whole business to gain, if he played the part of romantic lover. Yes, he was so good at it, and she was fooled!'

'You have no evidence of this, Mr Rorke. The court this morning has heard how deeply the accused felt for your daughter.'

Rorke lost control. He stood up, slammed a fist on the table and shouted, 'This man is rotten to the core. I want to see him hanged. Is that too much to ask?'

There were murmurs of support, but an official still had to play the right part, and force Rorke back to his seat.

'No further questions, Your Honour. This man is irrational, and he knows nothing of true love.' Raines enjoyed the smug feeling the words gave him. Rorke scowled back. He was marking the lawyer for vengeance as he took his seat back and tried hard to calm down.

SIX

He took the stage at first, so folk heard later. His story all came out later, when the adventure played itself out, finally. But Randal people often think back to the man and what he must have done and thought on that long journey west. It's one mighty long way from Galena, Illinois way out to the Rocky Mountains, and by stage it's slow as it gets.

Right, so he was not young any more, but he could handle a gun and ride a horse. He had sense enough to ask questions, and he was past the age when a man is fearful at the squeak of a rat or the howl of a wolf. His mission would override any of the little worries that best a traveller.

He would be stopping all the time. Horses and men have to be changed. Station after station comes along, and sure, there's maybe home cooking and a change in conversation. A man sure needs that. Being on stages, there's one great difficulty, and that's the brand of character you're shut in that box with. What if he came all that way, and sitting right next to him was a man with a stink about him, or some old tedious legal type who talked conveyances and wills for twenty hours?

But out he came, a man with a quest. He was a silent man: nobody never heard him start a conversation. If someone asked him, he would speak. Otherwise, he clammed up and went into his own thoughts. Course, he had plenty to think about. He was a man fixed on one aim, one target. Folk must have sensed that he was a man with a mission, but he was no preacher. He dressed in sober black. The way he looked invited speculation about his profession. Could have been a lawyer or a banker. Could have been a lawman. Was he by any chance one of them drifters that lives by the gun and has pistols and boot-guns concealed on his very dangerous person?

He told everything later, but before that he must have stared out at the endless flat of the Iowa and the Nebraska open land; he surely kept his mind busy with counting bison or maybe picking out strange formations in the floating clouds.

He was a card player. The folding lap-table came out and he played poker. That killed some time. He said later that for the first five days he had an old and a young woman with him, accompanied by a politician and a military man. They were suspicious of him, as he carried no more luggage than a small bag he kept with him all the time. He said that their eyes were always on his bag, pulled into curiosity by the mystery of what was in it.

One time, the politician asked him if he was a mountebank. 'We get mountebanks coming out west. They live on air and tall tales!' he said, inviting the company in the stage to chuckle with innocent pleasure. But he never smiled nor laughed. He had a face that was like leather, and found it too hard to crack and unwind. He had started out to put a stop to what might have been an unthinkable tragedy, and by heaven he was going to put his mind on that, and on nothing else.

Speaking to him much later, lawmen found him to be as hard to penetrate as a rockface. But then, he had more worries than most. Here was a man who set out on an epic journey, one in some ways tougher than the journey others going out west took, and he had no time for idle chatter. The women in the stage tried hard to lever out some opinions from him, even some comment about the latest entertainments that had been offered in Galena, as that was their home town, too. But no, he was like a castle with the drawbridge pulled up.

At least he played poker. But that matched his temperament perfectly. It didn't involve chatter. It entailed longish silences. Then he could sleep, or at least, pretend to sleep. He would prop himself into a corner, pull down his hat and create the snore that meant *stay away from me, say nothing to me. I am a man with something on his mind.*

The more miles the stage covered, the more pretend sleep he tried, and it gave him respite from the others. But he was too old to travel any other way, and too rich to worry about the cost.

The stage stop at what became North Platte by the railroad came as a mercy to him. He said that he paid the manager to have a bed in a shack away from his fellow travellers. Money opened up every door, he said. The men on top of the stage were more amenable to give him the right kind of talk. They spoke of the land, the critters, the Indians and the war brewing across the land touching the Oregon Trail. They made it clear that there was real danger, but they never said a word about it to the women.

Later, when he became a newspaperman for the Gallatin towns, he wrote about that journey, in which he made friends with the Gros Ventres people, and saw and heard the great movements of warriors around the Wyoming and Idaho territories.

But all this time he had only one thought. He didn't know that, should he ever find himself in the same room or under the same roof as his man, he could do what he vowed. He had that word *vow* always in his head. It drove him on. It gave him a reason to take another ride or drive or walk when his spirit was failing.

When citizens in Randal came to know him better later, after his arrival, he told them that there was nothing for him back home. The house he had built and furnished was empty but for three servants. The fences kept nothing in except memories of the dead. Once the rooms had been noisy with the shrill cries of children. But no more. In one summer, all life had been stifled there.

The ability to feel had gone. All the tears were shed. There had been more than enough wounds and blows dealt for one puny life to endure. If a blade sliced at his chest or a bullet cut into his heart, there would be nothing left in him to generate a response. Might as well shoot a dead man, he said to himself when, more than once, he faced probable death.

No, the quest was enough for any man, weak or strong. There was work to do and justice to mete out. He spoke about that later. His own story, in his paper, came from a grand old man, a leading citizen of Randal, Montana.

In the stage, days wore on, tedious as a Sunday sermon from a new minister. He coiled up even more into himself. Any answer he gave was restricted to one short, abrupt statement. A stage, he learned, was really a method of torture: a man had to squat in extreme discomfort for hours on hours, with other beings he hated or resented, and then worst of all, his body was subjected to physical pain in every bone. He began to understand the old classic tales about the medieval times when poor miscreants were put on the rack to have their limbs stretched.

He was that gunslinger they all suspected in that stage, but nothing he did ever gave him away. He kept the long coat and the black vest on; leather and bullet pouches were well hidden. What he was planning for could mean a storm of bullets or maybe no more than pressure applied by fear. He hoped it would be the second option. If it had to be slugs and blood, then so be it. He was ready to take the last ride, to the bosom of Abraham.

This is all that folk read, anyway, later on, and it was a tough read. His ordeal had made him a stone, a man without feeling. He would be capable of anything.

The younger woman in the stage making its way along the Platte, after many days in the bone-shaker, made him an offer. She was running the entertainment in a new hotel in the Wyoming territory. It was a high-class place, she said, and she needed a man who could look after her and the establishment. She had persuaded herself that he was a gunman.

But no, through his eyes, she stank of corruption. Here was another fallen angel. There was only one true angel, and he had failed to care for her. He blamed himself, beat his conscience so that its bruises never stopped aching.

It was the blame that took away all his peace of mind. Now he had to dish out what the law had not done. The law needed some teeth, and he was going to bite with them. Then the conscience might leave off, and the remorse might leave him to grieve as other men did.

One time at a station they were in trouble. A war party saw that there was easy prey out there, with just the passengers, two men atop and the station staff to oppose them. They tried to set fire to the main building and fired some shots into the windows. The manager and the stage driver barked out their orders, and the women were put safely under cover. The Indians thought it was going to be a good day for them until he went at them, a revolver in each holster and a sawn-down shotgun in his hands. He ran out, facing death in the poor light, and blasted at the nearest rider. He brought down three of the attackers and yelled at them so fiercely that they high-tailed it. The station master said the Indians thought a spirit-fighter had come from the dead to face them.

That was the man on his way to Randal. When he staggered back into the station hut they applauded him. He used to talk and write of that attack. He argued that it was when he was saved by the Almighty for his true work on earth. He told them all that he found faith that day, and that is what made him the rig'.. man to be the teeth of the law.

Later, he reached the end of the road as far as the stage was needed. He bought a horse. It was a fine, sturdy bay mare and he knew that he was paying far too much for her. He travelled as light as possible, hitting out from Case Ferry, leaving a disappointed woman behind, and a bunch of folks who thought they had met a character to match some of the old mountain men of the legends.

He never thought about himself, but the truth was he was beginning to look like a character from the old tales. His hair grew long and his beard was left to bunch up. He lost weight, and was thin and spare when he landed himself in the midst of the Rockies, relying on his guns to eat, shooting anything that moved. He acquired the art of disappearing into stones, creeks, grass and brush. But he rode in and out of the marked trail where wagons had gone, and lived in hope that his destination was coming closer. He almost started to believe that he could smell and hear like a native of that pure, clean, daunting land.

He was closing in. But he must have thought that fate was against him. He wrote later that he was found by some Gros Ventres. He was in a very poor state, *most near to the pearly gates* as he told us later. The Indians took him in, warmed him and fed him, as he related it, sip by sip over many days. He told the papers he could recall shivering so much that he thought he would never take a steady step again, nor take a normal breath.

He was left with an old couple in their tepee, and he gave a shaky memory of hearing them sing to him, and shake something so that it sounded like a sleigh-bell. Time and time again, when he was back in the world and found strength in his limbs again, he said that the will to put things right kept him alive. *I kept my mind on his face and on her face and I told myself I was a coward, but that it was not too late to set things right. No, sir, not too late.*

People reading his memoirs years later could only sit back, mouths agape with wonder and astonishment at the way he survived. Truth is, he lost the use of one of his feet. The Indians, he wrote, were better men of medicine and nursing than anybody he had ever met who wore a sober dark suit and charged big dollars.

He lost a deal of time over that injury. He fell behind, but he was a changed man. The man who set off north again after being so cared for was someone who had faith as well as justice in him.

He was still a strange mix, though. He was partly a hunter and partly a man out to deal his justice, to do what the law should have done, or what he should have done, years back. His friend Sky used to say that there's nobody knows the law like the man who breaks it with regularity.

Then came the day when his luck turned. He was in a broken-down old saloon, no more than a sod-house with a lean-to and a supply of rot-gut whisky. He sat at a table and there, opposite, was a man who looked to be as far down the ladder as possible. He stank of booze and desperation, and he wanted money. They got talking, and the man gave his name as Docherty. The traveller thought that maybe this man would be a useful security on the journey. He looked like he could take anything he wanted, and never ask for anything. He offered him ten dollars a day and it was accepted. The man would help him make it to Randal, where there was destiny waiting.

'I'm Bill Davey,' he told Docherty, 'and I got something to put right.'

SEVEN

Judge Baker had listened to too many accounts of how good a young man the accused had been, back in the murky past. Jed Raines had scoured the place for folk who knew his client. Baker had had enough by an hour after noon, and he called time out for eats.

Sheriff Hamer was only too glad to take some time out from the courthouse madness, as he saw it. The whole business was becoming too much to handle. He needed help, and that was to be found inside the church.

The minister was sitting at a table in a corner when Hamer came in, and he looked across at the lawman, who was one of his oldest friends. Just by looking at the man's face, Padre John knew he was needed. He stood up and held out a hand.

'Jack, Jack, you all right?'

Hamer looked his friend in the eyes. 'No, not at all, John. I need some advice.'

The minister sat his friend down at the table, where he had been writing a sermon.

The padre was a man that the locals joked lived on air. It was said that a strong breeze would blow him away. He was spare, lightly built, with his sandy hair brushed back. For man of fifty, he still had a boyish face, full of enthusiasm and life.

'Jack, I've not seen you here for some time, old friend.'

'No, Padre John, I lost a whole mess of things, mostly somethin' that you can't buy nowhere. I mean my self-respect. I guess I can't pray any more. I stopped believin' there's a God up there beyond them clouds, who's takin' care of me. He never took no care of my kin. No, John, I can't pray with my heart now. I'd be lyin' if I tried.'

The padre reached into a desk drawer and brought out a whisky bottle. 'John, take a swig and then speak out. You keep this in, and you'll be a sick man.'

'Yeah, sick is the right word, old friend. You see, I been weak. Weaker than a man should ever be. I let someone walk over me, push me away from the right road. Time was, I stood up to bullies, and to any kind of power misplaced...'

'Jack, are you talking about Rorke?'

Hamer took a swig of the whisky.

The padre saw his friend nod his head and pull a face of pain before he replied. 'John, I used to be a real lawman. Now I'm a skivvy. I might as well be a boot-boy. Fact is, when I lost my family, there I was, driftin' and lookin' for somethin' new. The man made it all sound like a new life with a deal of right thinkin.' I now see that he's greedy as the first pig to the teat.'

The minister stood up and took a few steps towards the light from his side-window. 'You know Jack, I know, more than most, what strength you got in there. It's not too late to put things right. I can tell you that. The dog that is whipped for too long eventually turns and bites the oppressor. Go and bite back, my friend.'

'You're right. Only pity is, there's an innocent man down the road, and he's about to swing in a few days, and what am I doin' about that? Nothin'. In fact, I'm keeping him down.'

'Turn and bite, Jack.' Padre John sat down again. 'Jack, when I came here and met you for the first time, you were fighting in the street. That was before you were a lawman. Remember? You were swinging your fists at a drunken man who was rip-ping at a lady's dress. I knew then that you were the right mind of man, the kind Randal needs, and needs real bad now.'

Jack Hamer brought that incident to mind. He saw his own face as it was that day, and he saw the woman being assaulted. The drunk had been floored and carried to the jailhouse by four good citizens. A week after that, Jack Hamer became a deputy. He had done the right thing time and time again, until Rorke started his threats and promises. It was like a black cloud had settled over the place and nothing would shift it. He got up, shook the hand of Padre John, and went out into the light. Was he going to act? Could he turn and change things? If he believed in prayer, he would have tried.

Hamer looked down the street. There was a strange silence about the place. It made him uneasy. Usually when there was quiet in the middle of the day, some kind of hell was like to break loose. The heat of the day turned some brains, he always thought. Yet for a few minutes, he looked at Randal and imagined he saw the town it used to be five years back: all raw and fresh, buildings just going up. There had been a long stretch of dance halls back then, and classier whore-houses. All that had been crushed and stopped by Rorke. The man didn't want laughter, somehow. Now, all that misery he carried around was made worse after his beloved Sarah died.

There was a wind whipping up, and a storm looked likely. Planks rattled and the brush rustled; horses were stirring and being restless. But still it was quiet, until there was a lone man on the move. He came out of the *Clarion* office with papers in his hands. It was Gotty Wellman. He had to pass Frank Hamer, and as he did, he stopped and said, 'Sheriff, guess who we got stayin' in The Gold Bullet?'

'Well, I can't read minds, Gotty. Tell me.'

'In that saloon, right now, there's Sky Davey. He's sittin' there eating beef and laughing at Kate's stories. I think she likes the man... but she don't know it's Sky Davey. This is a man who's taken twenty or more lives. He's a damned bounty hunter.'

Gotty ran on, grasping the papers to stop the wind from whisking them away. Hamer ran that name around in his head for a while, and then it all came back: the murders down the way towards Bozeman; the body of Jess Taylor at his place down Bannack. Word was that Sky Davey had been seen in the vicinity in both cases. Some said he was with the gang that robbed the stage a month back, but nothing was ever proved.

He could hardly walk in and arrest the man. There was no proof he had done anything. The territory was swimming in supposed villains and bandits, all with their bloated reputations, and with young bucks looking to take them on and be the next celebrated gunslinger. They all ended up in the graveyards, some sooner than others, but that's where they all were destined to be, some day soon.

Hamer had been nerved by Padre John. Half of him wanted to walk into the court, take Serlich out and back to his cell, and wait for a new trial – one without Baker running things. He was rotten as a tub of last year's fruit. But that was just half of him. The other half needed a drink.

He decided to follow Gotty and take a peep into The Gold Bullet, just to check on the Davey character. He would be no more than ordinary. They always were. Reputations shifted like sagebrush, and went off into the great emptiness where everything was forgotten, even heroes.

In the saloon of The Gold Bullet, the stranger and Kate had finished their meal and the card game had resumed, along with the old-timers by the window, who were back in the comfort of their scandal. But then Gotty scurried in, sat by his brother, and took out the sheets to show Harry. 'It's him, Harry... the stranger... it's Sky Davey. He's here to kill, you can be sure.' He whispered this and shoved the top sheet across the table, with its drawing of Davey's face very clear. Harry murmured the paragraph aloud, but kept it down: '*Sky Davey, the notable vigilante and gunman, shot down the two Royo brothers in Virginia City last Monday evening. Our report says they insulted him and challenged him to fight. Davey warned them not to try his patience, and when one spat at him, he drew both his pistols and put slugs in their hearts. Their hands never reached their holsters. Our reporter there says that Davey is in town to help some miners who are under threat from a gang.*'

'Read further down, Harry... he was there with his father, Bill. Seems they work together... or used to, anyway.'

Harry looked across at the stranger and checked his face with the drawing in front of him. 'Sure is him, and we have to write this up. He's here for a reason – a bad one, Gotty!'

'Yeah, that man is not Mr James Kamer. He's a liar as well as a killer.'

'What if he's here for the trial, Gotty?' Harry asked.

'If he's here for the trial, we need to watch him like a hawk!'

The stranger was now stretching out his legs, lying between two chairs, and watching the main door, as his hat flopped partly over his face. Nobody in the saloon dared to disturb him.

'If he's here to take a life,' Harry said, 'Surely it's no coincidence that there's the trial on. Maybe he's working for Rorke?'

'A man like that would be working for the Devil, you can bet on it. Rorke's the closest thing we got in Randal to Old Nick himself.'

'Well, Gotty… tell the sheriff!'

'I have done… he's not too keen on trouble. He runs away from it.' Gotty smiled wryly.

'Let's pray then, brother, and get the story written: *Gunslinger in town – why?*'

Jack Hamer watched through the front window, taking it all in. But he couldn't make out where Sky Davey was. Someone shouted for him. The court was back in session.

EIGHT

He was riding with Docherty, but after only a few miles, he sensed trouble. The man was dangerous and could not be trusted with the slightest thing. Docherty moaned and complained every time he was asked to do something. The first day together passed with Docherty talking only about what was wrong, what he didn't have, and why he got mixed up with an old-timer who was lost?

For the first few miles Docherty had said, 'Hey, mister, you got a good man here. Why, I been one of the best servants this side of the Mississippi. Yeah, sure, I been a lawman and I been a cowpuncher. I deserve the best pay you can afford. I can see you're a man of means!'

'I employed you to help me if I came under attack, Mr Docherty. I simply require you to fire your gun at any desperate type who comes at us. Understood?'

Docherty said he did, but sullenly. Somehow this new companion had to go. On the second day they fell out, and he told Docherty he was finished. 'You can go, I'm finished with you. Here's ten dollars. You're paid off.'

Docherty's hand was hovering over his revolver. The traveller saw it, and stood firm, looking him straight in the eyes. 'It's nearly dark. I'll camp tonight and leave in the morning.' Docherty said.

That night they were close to going across a tight pass. There was a narrow path ahead, and they camped by some low trees and brush above a creek. They were high, though, and it felt like a safe place. So it was, from predators at least. But he knew that he was not safe from Docherty.

As darkness closed in, he lay under his blanket, fully dressed, with his little boot-pistol held tightly at his midriff. Then he fought sleep. There was no doubt that Docherty knew there was a heap of cash to be taken from the old man who had taken him on. He had seen Docherty's eyes look around, searching out packs, pockets, leather saddlebags.

Some time around early dawn, just as the first flicker of light touches leaves with orange, he heard Docherty move. He sensed the movement, and then from the corner of one eye, there he saw the man stand and his hand go to his waist. It was a matter of seconds before the man would strike. There was a slight movement of shadow across the edge of the path where he lay, and he pushed aside the blanket, looked upwards and as he saw the flash of a blade, he fired the boot pistol. The bullet ripped into Docherty and the would-be killer fell back, rolling to the edge of the pass.

He scrambled to his feet. 'First death,' he told himself. 'Over you go, to the devil your master!'

From then on, he was on his own again, and vowed to stay that way. Docherty had proved that no one could be trusted. West of Kearny, he told himself, it was every man for himself, and morality was thrown away with the night soil.

He had made his first killing. At first it disturbed his thoughts, but then, the more he reflected on what had happened, the more he started to think of murder as something no more extraordinary as hammering in a nail or fixing a loose door. It was a job that had to be done. Docherty was aiming to put a knife in him and roll *him* over the edge down the deep valley side.

Still, it had been a very useful meeting. Docherty had told him about Randal, and he had met Rorke, whom he said was a cheating bastard. Yes, he was on the right track. There would surely be more dead men littering the track as time went on. He was in wild country.

He had a setback. One time, pushing himself too much, somewhere around Fort Hall but too far away from any settlement for anything or anyone to hear his cries except the predators, he fell and twisted his leg so bad that he had to lie still and do nothing. He had been leading his mare through a narrow defile when it happened. It was just a roll on a loose rock and down he went.

In his mind he saw the pictures he had seen in magazines about the frontier: the pioneer goes down injured and lies there helpless. Then along comes a grizzly, and the victim has only a knife to fend off the giant. The victim is easily taken and chewed up. Such was the punishment given by the wild to the fools who venture there alone.

That's what he had done, and he wrote about it later. Most of the west would know his story. They would know how he lasted out that night lying by the mare, covered in everything he could pull from his saddlebags. His teeth still chattered. There was no possibility of making a fire. But he came through. The next day he felt half dead, but there was a triumph that he had somehow been blooded, branded as a genuine frontiersman.

He was fit to help his son face the devil Rorke.

Now he was kept going by the drink. More and more, he relied on his whisky supplies, swigging some as he rode along, at times losing all concentration. One time he slipped from his horse and cracked his head on the surface of the hard earth. That taught him a lesson. But at night he did the drinking, sinking a bottle of the red nectar as some called it. The booze gradually seeped into him, so that more than once he stopped, curled up somewhere in any kind of shade, and slept.

He sensed that there was something deeply wrong: he just *knew* it. Lying alone in the dark, hearing only the coyotes or the wolves, he would have a feeling that he was on a mission to put things right. Too long he had sat back and let things slip. Yes, he was responsible for all the wrong, all the cruelty. There was a situation to be put right. There was some punishment due. Would he have the courage to face the criminal and gun him down like a dog?

The rage was building up. The more time passed in the frustration of being alone and helpless in that wilderness, the more he felt the anger down inside, like a dark pool of hatred, waiting for its release, when it would flood out and engulf everyone near. It was such a limbo, such a helpless waiting in the wings, this lonesome journeying across the known world and into the American desert. But now he was sniffing on the wind the prey he sought.

. The time was coming when he would strike: he was planning a dramatic arrival, to match the seriousness of the story he had come to close, to finish. He was the lawgiver who would bring punishment and fair judgement on the guilty. The worst of it was that his own blood had turned rotten. His own blood had made his name stink. They would all know, back home where his name counted for something, they would know and they would speak of him in nasty tones, bringing his name down, making him no better than an outlaw.

But for now he chewed on hardtack and fried jack rabbit, and he lived like some wandering priest. He was the man chosen to show the law how it should and could deal out the verdicts against the lowest of the low in that shameless, lost land. Of course, he had to do all this alone. No other man could be trusted to act with him or for him. This was a task allotted to him by the Almighty. Even more than that, it was something he had to do to win back his good name. When he had the proof of his justice, he would carry back the sinner to his own land. The sinner might be his own blood, but that meant nothing: what mattered was that he was seen to be putting things right.

Yes, the day was near. Let them shiver in their guilt and sin. Let them run to find help with the Devil, but he would turn away. He would fade and he would run for the cover of night. The Devil himself would not face the wrath coming at his spawn. He, the dealer of justice, had strength in his arms to match and defeat the whole of the Devil's army of fallen angels. Lying in the darkness and stillness of the night out in Idaho, he felt the strength streaming into his limbs, making the core of his being a force to match any Satanic brood set on him.

Even with the whisky sunk into him, cramping his brain and slowing down all his actions, he kept his aim true and forced himself on. He had always been resolute. He always knew what he wanted from life. That toughness was still in him, in spite of the strong drink filtering through to his limbs and his maimed thinking.

NINE

Jack Hamer took advantage of a short recess at the court to walk across the street and call on Kate. She was behind the bar, helping the barman gather the rubbish from the previous night. When Jack walked in and sat at the end of the bar, she went over to him.

He tipped his hat and gave her a smile. He felt good just being with her. 'Kate, would you have just a little greeting for a lawman with problems?'

'Just an excuse for a kiss on the cheek, Jack Hamer,' she said, as she pecked him on the cheek, and then slid a beer across the counter for him.

'Cal not here?' Hamer asked, hoping he wasn't.

'Still on the road. I have no notion of where the man goes. He says it's to do a deal and make us so rich that we'll have three hotels. Do I believe him? No.'

'Well, there's more money in his line of property work than in keeping the law.' Hamer was always adept at hiding his true feelings. Now he gave the woman a succession of loving glances as she scribbled something on a list. 'Things to do, Jack… never do hotel work. You're always running short of something.'

'One thing *you* will never be short of, Kate… is love.'

She looked up from her list and studied his face. Was he hinting again, hinting about something he needed to say? Then he laughed it off, finished the beer, and said, 'Kate, you need to know one thing for sure… any time you need me, just holler. I'll hear ya holler. You know why? Because I'm listening for your voice all the time, hoping that you will walk right on in and give me that smile you have that chases all the troubles of life away.'

'I'll holler!' she said, putting a hand over his on the bar counter. For a moment, their faces came close. But the feeling dissolved as a voice called out.

'You got a minute, Kate?'

Kate de Giles was needed upstairs, where her three girl dancers were preparing for an entertainment that night, so their talk was cut short. They wanted to show her what they had come up with, as it was Cal Delano's birthday and he was expected home soon. In fact, he had been expected two days back, and Kate was trying not to worry about it.

She loved the talk with the stranger, who was a true gentleman and the best company a woman could want, but when she had to go, he strode over to the window and found a seat where he could watch the courthouse. Kate knew that she liked the company of men, but in her younger days that had almost been her ruin. Back in Denver, as a young woman going west and losing her brother and some friends, she had ended up on her own in a city that thrived on whore-houses and small hotels dressed up to look classy, when really they were no better than brothels.

Now today, the girls had a wonderful routine worked out. Kate sat in a deep armchair and watched as they walked around, lifting their skirts, imitating the movements they would actually make on the stage downstairs, at the back of The Gold Bullet. When they finished the first run-through, with old Pete Rund at the piano, they stood in a line and bowed, with smiles sweet enough to win the hearts of the most ornery old cuss.

'That's just right, girls! He will love it. Pete, you should have been a concert pianist at some swell place back east, you hear?'

Pete gave her a smile and a little bow.

Clara, the lead dancer, who taught the others how to move gracefully and without stamping like steers, tapped Pete on the head and then kissed his cheek.

'He's a real professional, Miss Kate. You know, you should get some actors out here and put on a play!' The other girls called out in agreement. They were a lively bunch, young and ready for fun. It made Kate's heart feel young as well, when she was with them.

'I'm real pleased… carry on, girls. Let's make Cal have the best day of his life. He's thirty years old, though I joke that he was born sixty. He's so serious!'

'We love him,' Clara said, with a giggle, 'We love to tease him. You should marry him, Miss Kate. You're so good together, right girls?'

They called out again, echoing her words.

Kate was failing to hide her concern, though. Cal was two days overdue. He had been down in Wyoming trying to collect some money he was owed, and maybe there was trouble. She had hated the way he kept making business deals in all sorts of places. He dreamed of being as rich as Declan Rorke, and he looked up to the man like some sort of father that Cal had never had. He had been an orphan, taken in by a religious family back in New York, but had headed out west with a wagon train. He had just run away as soon as he was fifteen and could handle himself. Now here he was, causing her some serious worry.

She wasn't dealing well with all the anxiety he brought to her. Their two years together had been an up-and-down affair, mainly because he was away from home so often, and for so long. 'It'll all be worth it, sweet, you wait and see. We'll live like king and queen!' That's what he said, time and time again, and he was too proud to work with anybody else. Now here he was, hundreds of miles away, and could have been killed or maimed for all she knew.

He was fair, bearded and agile, active as a mountain goat, she always said, when she laughed at him. He carried no weight, and was all muscle. He could have run all day, chasing quarry. He was maybe the best man with horses around Randal too, and he could have earned plenty by staying at home and working around the town. He had no interest in hotels and fine things, and he wanted to be on the road. He was hungry for something, and that something was always at the end of the next valley or over the next mountain.

Kate went to her boudoir and sat at the dressing-table. She would keep herself looking good for when he did come home. There she was, looking at herself in the mirror, noticing every line around the eyes or by her mouth: it was tough, keeping up the right kind of appearance. The toughest thing about her life was keeping The Gold Bullet clean and free – that is, clear of Rorke and his associates. They wanted the place. Their offers had been turned down, time and time again. She knew that the man had to be faced, stood up to, looked in the eye.

The fight took its toll. She opened a drawer and took out the bottle of brandy. One glass was poured, and knocked back. The glass was filled again. The warm feeling it gave her brought some desperate cheer. It was all down to the loneliness. She had a lonesome life, but it never had to show. She drank the third glass and then whispered to herself: 'There she sits, the drunk from Denver, still tainted by the whore-house!'

Then she needed sleep. The drowsiness came over her and made her drop forward, head down on the table top, resting on her arms. Not a soul could say that she was lonesome. She smiled at the world. 'Cal, come home, come home now! I need you...' she said, mumbling the words into her sleeved arm, and ragging her heavy head to one side, where she could not see herself any longer in that hateful glass.

With an effort, she forced herself to sit back then, and brushed her hair. She had to look good for Cal. He could ride into town at any time. She was working hard to be happy with him, but it was still mostly a struggle on her own, the way it had always been for her. She had learned to expect nothing from men except problems, and Cal was no different, but what *was* different was that he tried too hard, worked too intensely, to see that he was not spending enough time with her. He left her to the hotel and the saloon for too long.

But she pulled herself together, and she set about making more preparations. There was food to prepare, and maybe it was time she wrapped that little gift of some fine new watercolours she had bought from the dealer in town who helped the wealthier folk to decorate their homes. Cal had plans for a new house for them, a short way out of town, with plenty of land, and the watercolours would be for that when it was done.

Downstairs, the stranger, James Kamer, was keeping his distance from the rest, and they were all chatting and card playing, watching him from the corners of their eyes – but the peace was about to be disturbed by Gotty and Harry, who were now sitting in a corner, looking through the papers and pictures from Wyoming papers and beyond, and they were now sure that the man out there was not Kamer, but a killer for hire. He was not the kind of man that Randal wanted to encourage

When they walked out, holding a sheet with a picture of Kamer on it, they first met Kate and told her: 'Miss Kate, see this. Look who your new friend really is! You been associating with a known killer and a thoroughly undesirable type!' Gotty spoke fast, anxious as usual to be heard and to influence others to see the world his way.

Kate took a look, and then glanced over at the man relaxing by the window, and her face changed its expression. 'It's him, boys! But you know, he's done no harm. Anyhow, do we believe the papers? I never believe your *Clarion*, to be truthful. We all know you stretch the truth to fit what you want the world to see. Come on, now, you know that's true!'

'He's not wanted,' Harry said.

'Well, you going to tell him to go?' Kate smiled.

The brothers looked at each other. Gotty said, 'Maybe not, but I'm aiming to tell these good folks about him.'

'Go ahead. But be warned,' Kate said, 'He might not like it.'

Gotty walked out into the saloon, with Harry behind, and he held up the sheet of paper. 'My friends, could I have your attention for a moment?'

They all looked at him.

'Now see, I'm holding up some proof that the man over there, the stranger that Kate has just been dining with, and who you all welcomed real hearty like, that man is not James Kamer, as he says he is. No, he is a man known as Sky Davey, and he kills folk for a living. Admit it sir, you're a bounty hunter and a gun for hire.'

Heads turned, and all the attention of the saloon was on the man lounging in the chair. He now sat up and looked across at Gotty. Then he stood up. 'Well now, I can't argue with that. You got me. I hardly wanted you good Montana people to know that I was Sky, did I? I might be here to do a job. That job might be to remove one of you from this earth.'

There was some shuffling and murmuring around the saloon.

'It might be,' he went on, 'But I'm not gonna tell you. It's my business. Now if you think it's illegal for a man to give a false name and sit down all well behaved and such, then go get your lawman. Maybe one of you wants to hurl me out of this place? Yeah? That right?'

There was more uneasy shuffling.

'Right. If you've nothing else to say, then let's get on.'

'Hold on, mister.' Harry cut in now: 'You're dodging the point here. You're watching the courthouse like a hawk. There's a trial going on, and a man's life is under threat. You're a killer and you're watching the front of that courthouse. Even a less than average smart man could figure that you got *designs*.'

The tall man smiled and had to stop himself laughing. 'Designs? You like to elaborate?'

Gotty joined in. 'I'll explain. You're here to prevent justice, right? You been assigned to shoot dead Bill Serlich. Now, if the man is guilty, he will hang and...'

'Hey, slow down, mister.' The stranger said, raising a hand. 'Look, I'm not here to kill any man called Serlich. I never heard the name. Fact is, I'm here to meet somebody – my Pa. He's on his way right now. We're meeting here, and that's all I'm telling you. My life and what I do is nobody else's business. You got that? You're a typical, interfering', annoyin' newsman. I met plenty of 'em. Get back to your printing press and leave us folk to take it easy here.'

The Wellman brothers sat down. Kate offered some free drinks to them to help the situation. But the old-timers were not satisfied. Dandy called out, 'A killer don't come here just to stare at a building. Anyway, we got a right to know who you really are.'

'Old man, I am indeed the man known as Sky Davey. But that's all you're gonna get from me. Now sit down and do some gossip or I might consider you annoying, and that means I'd have to knock you through one of them walls.'

There was a hush for a while as normality returned, and then Kate had her words to say to the stranger, and she said them quietly, sitting next to him. 'Look, so you are Sky Davey, and I'm happy to call you Sky. All I want to say is that if you're peaceful and straight with life, stay here like the guest you are. My man's due back soon and it's his birthday. You're welcome to take some drinks and food with us when he comes. All I ask is that you don't indulge in your profession inside these walls.'

'I can assure you, Kate, that my business here involves nobody in this room.'

She was satisfied with that, and left him alone. Everyone in the saloon left him alone after that. The Wellmans were already writing out their feature eon him, and Gotty was doing a sketch of the man, in profile, ready for the next edition of the *Clarion*.

Things seemed back to normal, though Dandy was cursing and swearing under his breath for the next hour.

TEN

The young man watched the other jurymen eat and drink, sitting along the table at the back of the room, enjoying a laugh and a story about the man who stood accused. It revolted him to see this, and the more he stared at them, the more he saw them as repulsive animals, heartless, corrupt beasts who had no right to sit in judgement. He decided that something had to be said and he jumped to his feet, throwing a plate of food on to the floor. They could see that his rage was dangerous, and they sat back, defensively.

'You men, you disgust me! You take dollars to ensure a death, and the man out there may well be innocent. You are disgusting as swine!'

'What's the matter sonny, did Rorke's man never get to you? You got no bankroll I guess?' This was from the chairman of the jury, a man who sweetened and strained with every move, so gross was his old body. Sitting there, stuffing his face, his breathing could be heard several feet away, and his one aim in life appeared to be to stir up trouble and poke fun.

The young man went on, 'I might be a fool, but I believe in justice, and I believe in law. These things are there to see that the right is preserved and that the good, upright man is protected. You men are taking dollars to ensure that a man hangs. Well, I'm about to tell the judge all this... I seen what's happened.'

There was general laughter. The chairman stood up, walked over to the young man and put an arm around him, 'Now son, let me explain how life works here in Randal. You see things have a way of not going a man's way. The most evil rogues get clean away with their dark deeds, because the law has gaps in it... gaps made by folks like you who want every little thing in life to be clean and shiny as a new coin. Truth is, the law has a way of being filthy and repulsive as a flee-blown carcass. You see the point? That being so, then right-minded men have to make sure that scum like Serlich gets what they deserve. You can see that, surely? The man stood in court and told a pack o' lies. In truth he shot down them young people in cold blood. Mr Rorke wants a decent, lawful world, and he's willing to pay for it.'

He took away his hand, and then looked the young man in the eyes.

'Thanks for all that twisted thinking mister. My name is Joel Borne, and I have the strange belief that a jury should have its own mind, and do the right thing.'

The chairman turned to his friends, 'We have a little prig here, men. What are we to do?' They sniggered at that.

Nothing more could be said, as they were soon to be called back into the court. But Joel Borne was determined to act, to do something. They would all sit down, along with the citizens of Randal, and then the lawyers and Judge Baker, an they would kill justice stone dead. Joel felt his anger rising in his breast, a rage that was going to burst out, and tell the world that a terrible injustice was happening.

There was only one thing he could do, and that was find Sheriff Hamer and tell him what was happening. He walked through towards the washroom and then ducked into a corridor, where he should not have been, and went to find the lawmen.

They were sitting in the next room to Serlich, who sat with his lawyer, Raines. Jack Hamer and Ry were finishing off their meal, and as Ry wiped his mouth with his bandanna, Joel knocked on the door, which was half open, and asked if he could come in.

'Sure. What do you want, son?'

'I need to speak to you, sheriff, on a most urgent matter.'

Ry stood up and went out to find something to do. It might have been a private matter. Then Jack Hamer waved towards an empty chair. The young man sat there, nervous and more than a little overawed.

'I don't know what to say and how to start, sheriff, but I'm here with something important to say. I'm a member of the jury for this case, as you know, and well, you are the only person I can speak to. I don't know how far this rotten business extends. Maybe it digs deep in this little town, like a red sore, biting deep.'

Hamer was worried. He sensed that the kind was on to something and that it was going to be an uncomfortable situation. 'Spit it out, kid... what's your name?'

'Joel, sir... Joel Borne.'

'How old are you, Joel?'

'Young, but old enough to know corruption when I see it!' Now he was turning red in the face and starting to lose control. Whatever he was holding in, it was now slipping out and he was speaking too fast.

'Slow down, Joel, easy now. Just gather your thoughts and your words and then tell me, slowly and carefully, why you came to see me.'

'Sure... sure. You see, Mr Hamer, I seen the jury members accepting bribes! I seen it with my own eyes.'

Jack Hamer's heart sank. It was Rorke again. It was yet another abuse, another lousy and bent piece of chicanery. But Hamer knew he sat there as a bought man. He was as rotten as the jurymen.

Yet there he sat, putting on an act. How much of this was he going to take? How could Rorke be stopped?

'Son, you say you saw this? Who gave out the money?'

'The chairman... it's from Declan Rorke. Anybody can see that, sir!'

'Yes, sure. But there's no proof. If you had proof, I could act.' Hamer felt himself hating the words as he spoke them. 'Get me proof, right? If this is happening, then it could be deeply wrong. I know that. The man has been watched for some time.'

'Watched? So you suspect him of foul play? Sheriff, surely you could arrest him?'

His face changed then. Hamer could see it. The kid's face dropped, sank down, as he realized a terrible truth. It took a while for him to find the right words, but finally he said, 'Sheriff Hamer... *you're* taking dollars from the man... aren't you?'

Hamer's face was still as a stone. He showed no response and no emotion.

'You *are*. I see it in your face, plain as day.'

Joel Borne ran off, slapping a fist against a wall in frustration and rage as he went back towards the jury room.

Hamer sat there, his head down, his mind running through all the doubts he had in him. A kid had seen in him the worst, stinking bent, crooked soul that was in him now, and there he was, still walking around with the tin star on his breast.

When Ry came back he saw that something was wrong. Now, Ry had no knowledge of anything Jack Hamer was doing. The sheriff always kept a tight lip and dark secrets in the dark and no place else.

'It's nothin' Ry. Time to get him back in the court.'

In the office of the *Clarion*, Harry and Gotty Wellman were putting together their feature on the stranger, the man they were sure was Sky Davey. Gotty was writing the piece and Harry was searching through more cuttings and records. 'It has to be him, Gotty… it's him, for sure… right?' Harry read everything real fast, jotting down some key phrases to be used.

'It's the killer, I'd bet my life on it, brother. Now, I'm saying "ruthless murderer" and I guess that's in the headline. Right?'

'Murderer is better than "killer" I guess. One thing though, brother,' Gotty said, 'When this is in print… what's he gonna do? He gonna come lookin' for us?'

'If he does, we have verification.'

'Verification? Oh, that'll be fine in our graves. We can be two corpses shouting out that we were killed by Sky Davey. Use your brain, brother!' He stared at Harry as if his brother had lost his brain.

But the piece shaped up. It was nothing but sensation and drama – words packed through with fear and panic.

A while later, when the trial was underway again, the brothers returned to The Gold Bullet. They had to see and hear everything, and most of all they had to watch the stranger like he was a snake in the hands, ready to wriggle away at any time. When they walked in, there was nothing more than the restrained mumbling chatter of drinkers and gamblers, except for noises and voices from the back room where the stage was busy with the ladies rehearsing, and the tables were being set up, under the supervision of Kate.

The newsmen went to a corner from where they could see Sky Davey and also the street beyond. The tall stranger had now come around from his dozing and was staring out at the courthouse. The newsmen, always observant, saw that one of the man's hands was now taking a revolver from its holster. He started to clean the gun, and then check the chambers, giving them a spin. A rifle by his side was also checked.

'He means business' Gotty said, 'But what business? I mean he's not here to register the rainy weather.' His brother said nothing except, 'Yeah. Who knows?'

The weather was beginning to be a factor in everything happening in Randal. Sheets of rain lashed against the walls and windows, right along the main street. The wind was rattling wood and making some shutters and roofs bend and flap.

Folk on the street held on to their hats and bent forward into the wind.

Kate, more worried than ever about her Cal, walked across the room and asked old Dandy if he could help her.

'Sure. What can I do?'

'I'm getting real concerned about my man. He should be home now, Dandy... he should be home!' She put her handkerchief to her eyes and wiped away a tear.

'What can I do, Kate? You see the storm out there. Maybe he's stopped to take cover... caught in that old wind, eh?' He put an arm around her.

'Dandy...as soon as it dies down, will you go and find him? He should be on the Bozeman road.'

'Sure will, my dear, sure will. Now you sit down and rest your feet. Rest your mind, even more important. Listen to old Dandy, now.'

She did listen. She sat down by the bar and asked for a brandy. It was the only thing that would help.

ELEVEN

He reached a point in the north Gallatin when folk told him that Randal was not too far. They told him it was maybe thirty miles north, and he just had to follow a river. One of the men he spoke to knew Rorke, and they pulled a frown when they said his name. He had asked around every time he stopped or when someone on the road passed him. He was making sure that he was closing in on Randal and on the chance to do the law's work.

It was as he set out from a homestead in the Gallatin that he was aware that a wagon was coming up close behind him, and as it came close and pulled alongside, the driver shouted across, 'Stop for coffee, friend?'

They did, and the man, bearded and weathered, around forty, with a full-bodied laugh and a keen sense of pleasure, sat down opposite Bill Davey and talked about his life. 'It's all about being smart, mister. Using this.' He tapped at his bald head. 'See, you need to think what folks need, find out where they are, and then supply what they need. Gettin' rich is real easy. Take my wagon – you know what's in it? Cats! It's full of cats!'

They stopped and rested, and the cats were explained. 'You get mining camps, right? You get folks diggin' holes. They have food scattered everywhere. Next thing you know – you got vermin! You need cats.'

'You're a trade then?' Bill Davey asked.

'Name's Sam Mirez. I've everything and anything. A man can hire me for whatever he wants. I'm headin' to Randal as I've heard there's work and a certain amount of trouble from the miners. I heard tell they make their own law...'

'Well, maybe so, but Mister Mirez, I guess you can fire straight?'

'You bet. I been on the cattle trails. I even fought the Comanche once. I lost, naturally. They always come out on top if there's horses and shootin' involved.'

'Well, before you've sold your cats, how would you like to work for me... just one little job? It's likely to be in the next week some time and I need a gunman.'

'Tell me more.'

'I'm on my way to Randal to meet up with my boy, and we have a score to settle. It's very simple. We have a man to nudge out of the world. A little bit of lead should do it.' He laughed so that his throaty cackle turned into a cough, and Mirez joined in. They were getting on like old friends.

'This man who has to meet his maker... what's he done that's so bad?'

'Never mind all that. Let's just say it involves my son's woman. Now, the offender in question should never mess with another man's woman, that's a general comment, but this time he messed with Sky Davey's woman.'

Mirez screwed up his leathery face and then let out a sound from his lips that conveyed something between a sigh and a chorus of 'Oh boy, he's doomed.' He looked Bill in the eyes, and said, 'So you're the father of Sky Davey? Reckon you had a handful there, bringin' up that wild one.'

'He's a good boy. Just has a temper.' Bill smiled wryly.

'Yeah. Me too.' Mirez finished his coffee. 'How much and what's the deal, Bill?

'Two hundred dollars for maybe an hour's work. You just have to wait for the man to walk in a street or come out of a store, somethin' like that, and then shoot him dead. Easy work.'

'Let's shake hands, Bill Davey!' Mirez shoved a plug of tobacco in his mouth, then shook hands, got to his feet, and said, 'Lead on. I'll follow you.'

Bill felt the craziness of the situation, riding on, close now to Randal, followed by this drifting gun for hire, and his wailing, mewling cats.

*

Back in court, the jury and the public were listening to Rorke's side of things. He was called by Teller, who was on his side.

'I came here with high hopes. Dreams. Plans. It's exactly the kind of town where a man can start again. I needed to do that. It's a long story, but to sum it up, I'd been through hard times and I had only the clothes I walked in and twenty dollars in my pocket. I'd been down before, and I'd been on the rise, too, and I knew how to claw back an identity, out west being the perfect place to do that. Out here a man can be what he wants, what he tells the world he is. It's not pretence, it's not fraud. It's a man rebuilding himself. You good folks of Randal can understand that. A year brought a measure of success. I was making money, got a wife, built a homestead. But there is always some low type who blows in like sagebrush and wants what you got. Bill Serlich was that low-life dirt.'

'What did he do, Mr Rorke?' Teller put on his most gentlemanly front.

'Serlich is the kind of man who has somethin' a decent man hates – he has charm. He sweet-talks the fair sex, and he seduces them. I seen him at work, believe me. He came into our lives, puttin' on a performance that he was going into politics and he was to be a big noise around Montana. We're talking about the kind of man who made enemies, I reckon. He has a skill in that.'

He was upset, or at least he put on an act of being upset. He and Teller knew that although they had the jury in their hands, the townsfolk had to be on his side, so that future dealings and talks would always have a degree of sympathy for the accused.

Teller made the most of the opportunity to gather sympathy. 'Mr Rorke, would you say that your daughter was seduced?'

Raines cut in, shouting, 'Your Honour, that's not an acceptable line...'

The judge waved a hand. Raines sat down.

Rorke put on a special frown for the sake of the court before answering. 'My daughter was shamefully taken in, as any woman would by this Lothario. He knew exactly what he was doing and...'

'Shut your lying mouth, Rorke!' This came from Serlich, who had to be restrained. Judge Baker then reprimanded him and he sat back, seething with a sense of injustice. Teller was back in his stride. 'Do carry on...'

'Well, Your Honour,' Rorke turned to look at Baker, and he thought of the roll of banknotes in the judge's pocket, 'My daughter was the model of purity and honesty. I believe that she gave in to his blandishments while under the influence of wine. He plied her with drink. She never drank, I swear...'

He stopped speaking as there was a shuffling in the ranks of the jury and someone was muttering and starting to curse. Suddenly, out on to the floor walked Joel Borne, raising a fist and staring at the judge. 'Your Honour, this travesty has to stop! I have evidence that there is corruption in this trial.'

'The young man is suffering from an unbalanced mind, Your Honour,' Teller put in.

Judge Baker waved his hand towards Jack Hamer, who walked across and grabbed the young man by the collar. Borne went on talking, 'You have to listen, you have to do something. This jury is being bribed I tell you, bribed!'

There were mutterings across the court. Most folk knew the young man very well. They all knew his family. He had never shown any sign of mental anguish or illness. Gossip had started. Then, as he was being carried away, Borne took something from his pocket and threw it at Declan Rorke. It was a knife, and there was a startled shout of fear from those who sat near enough to see it. The blade sank into the wood of the stand where Rorke stood, so close to his right hand that blood was drawn, in a thin line, across the side of his hand.

'There is blood, Your Honour' Teller called out. Judge Baker called for an adjournment and the court emptied, slowly, with a swelling tide of chatter and complaint.

In a back room, Jack Hamer sat with the boy while Ry watched Serlich next door. The town doctor, who was sitting in court, came around by the back entrance and looked at Rorke's hand. He saw Hamer and asked if he had arrested and charged Borne yet. Someone ran over the road to fetch one of the Wellman brothers, and Gotty was there within a few minutes, pressing to be let in at the back door.

Hamer took hold of Borne and walked him out of the room and towards the jail. He had to get him locked up. There was still a solid rainfall and a wind strong enough to break a fence. Behind him ran Gotty, asking questions at too fast a rate.

'What did he do, Jack? Has he been in a fight? What did he do?'

Hamer ignored him, and marched Borne straight into the office and then into a cell.

'Mr Wellman, I'm staying here a while. I'm locking the door.'

Gotty stood outside, notebook ready, and called out questions, louder than normal, so that heads turned as people walked by, going about their business.

*

In The Gold Bullet, Kate was still asking Dandy to go and find her man. The old-timer said he could, but only when the weather calmed down. Ready to comfort her was the stranger. He sat by her at the window-seat and tried to reassure her.

'Ma'am, your man, he'll most likely be held up by this storm. Right? Think about it. He's only maybe twenty miles away? Now, this rain and the wind from hell, they're most likely scootin' down the valley from Bozeman. They get stronger when they're channelled by the narrow valley. He'll be holed up some place, drinking and thinkin' about you. You know I'm right.' He squeezed her arm and then she ducked her head to one side as if she was about to rest it on his broad shoulder.

Everybody in the saloon saw that. Most were sure that Kate was a mite more than friendly to the tall stranger. Then news came from a kid assigned to update them all on the trial that everything had stopped. He stretched the truth. 'Folks, Mr Rorke, he got shot. There was blood. Some man in the room came at him, and there was blood on the wood. Mr Rorke is with the surgeon right now!'

After ten minutes of reporting and inventing, the whole saloon was thinking that Rorke was bleeding to death, and they figured that Bill Serlich did the deed. The only thing that could die down the talk of the sensation was more news, and Harry Wellman brought that. He walked in, looked across the room and pointed at the stranger, who was now sitting close to Kate and letting her weep a little.

'That man, over there. We know who he is. Yes, that man is none other than Sky Davey, and he has to be here for something bad! Come clean, Mr Davey, why are you here?'

Everyone stared at the man as he said, speaking real slow and steady, 'I admit I am Sky Davey. I am that man. But I'm just passin' through. Tomorrow I'll be on my way north.'

'You think we believe that?' Harry went on, 'You think we believe a word a killer might say? Why, you're the lowest critter around, lower than a rattler, taking gold for killin'. That's the Devil's work, if you ask me. You know folks, Gotty and I have proof of what this man has done, and you can read it in tomorrow's *Clarion*. It's all there, in print, what he did in California, and then the incident at Barrow Cross when three men were shot dead. Sky Davey was there at all these events, and we've tracked him down. Now here he sits, looking respectable, when the truth is he's a cold-blooded murderer. Do we want him in this town?'

There was no time for a reply, because Kate stood up. 'I don't believe it, Harry Wellman. You're being the newspaperman right now, whipping up a story, only it's as stretched as a washing line! I have got to know this man... Sky... and he's a gentleman. He's given me more help than all your people put together. Now as he's in my hotel, he's my friend, and if any of you want to see him arrested, then you have me to deal with. This man sitting by me is my new friend, and he's staying here!'

'Is he now? Your new friend?'

The question came from the front entrance, and the man who spoke the words was Cal Delano, wet and tired, standing there, gathering just enough strength to speak, but when he saw his woman tap the stranger on the shoulder, real affectionate, he found that there was passion in his heart, and his hand was hovering over his Colt.

TWELVE

Rich Seward signed in at the cheapest hotel in Randal. He was thin and weary from a long ride all the way from Virginia City, and he was pretty much penniless. His last dollars paid for a room and a meal, and he was ready to ask around about the man he was here for.

He was young: barely twenty-two – and he was set on one thing. Everything else was a distraction. He had left home two years back, living by working with the cook on a cattle trail adventure. Then he had got into a fight with two cowpokes in some bum town in Kansas, and had gone west after gunning them down.

The past was not a part of his life now. The past was to be forgotten. He had to make the future *mean* something. You had to have a *name*. He had learned one essential skill for survival: to instil fear into others when it was needed. He had learned a look, a threat, a tone of voice, all learned in the way a rat learns to fight its corner, defend its space.

He was fast on the draw. That he had learned. More than that, he had come to see that being neat with a gun could be a pleasant way to live and it got you noticed. All his life so far, till he learned to shoot, he had been talked down, pushed around, spat on. He had been a drifting orphan, abused by everyone. He had even slept out in a yard with stray dogs one time.

But not any more. He had faced out and killed a fancy gunslinger in Virginia City, and then helped a gang kick out some bullies from a seam. Now he saw the value of a reputation. He was in the lowest part of town, but he had his sights on a man who would increase the fear around Rich Seward ten times. He was in Randal for one thing – to kill the man who had left Virginia City just before him: Sky Davey.

Talking to the manager of the little hotel, he asked about Randal.

'Well, mister, you're in the part where the whores hang out. You see across the street, that line of hovels called Grey Bar? That's the whore street. Damn place stinks. You here, stayin' around this neck of the woods, then you're in bad times. You look like Lady Luck has kicked your backside. No offence, but what did you do wrong? You made enemies?'

'Sir, listen to me. I want you to remember who I am. My name is Rich Seward, and you are gonna know that name very well indeed before this week is over. Oh yes, Rich Seward. You can say, soon now, that Rich Seward stayed in your flea-pit one time, and you can tell the papers, and they'll pay you well, my friend.'

'That's big talk mister. You ain't nothin' more than five feet two and you look worn out. I have to speak as I see!'

'That's fine. I like an honest man. You got some heart in you to talk like that to a man who's took three lives.'

'Three lives?'

'Sure. Three lives. Fourth one comin' up. Now I need to take a walk and see this place before nightfall.'

He was short, wiry, swarthy. His features were strong and his face mean. He tended to scowl at the world, as it had always disappointed. Rich was a man with no roots. Brought up by any stray drifter, he had always lived short of sustenance and affection. A coyote was the closest thing he had to a friend, he used to joke, when in his whisky. He only knew, from rumours and odd remarks, that some folk thought his father was an Apache. He wanted to believe that. The Apache lived close to how he wanted to live. But for now, he had to rise in the world.

It was like a fallen world, he thought, this Randal town. Most of it was neglected, swept aside, so it could not embarrass the church-going folk. You passed a line at the end of a road with a broken-down stable, and suddenly there were true family homes, after streets of ramshackle huts and tents. Yes, it was a town of two very different colours. One was kinda pink and happy, and the other blue and dirty. Right now, he thought he was a denizen of the blue. Even after a bath, he felt dirty.

Passing a general store, he called in and asked about what was going on in the town. The fat man with his shiny white apron said that there was a big trial going on. Everybody in town talked about it. He had the full story from the fat man, who finally asked if there was anything he wanted from the store? Rich had nothing to spend, nothing at all. He managed a thank you and tipped his hat before he left. The one thing he did do was tell the man his name.

Every place in Randal knew Rich's name by the afternoon. They would all recall the young, unshaven man with the dark, tanned face and the fancy vest. That was his trademark – a shiny gold vest with two decorated pockets in which he kept his lucky medals. He had found these in Mexico when he was a small, weedy kid on the loose, and had kept them as lucky charms. They both had heads on them – maybe kings' heads. So far they had been lucky for him.

Paying for his horse to be fed and rested, then the hotel, had skinned him dry of any dollars at all. It was not a desirable state of affairs, so it was time, as dusk came on, to do some bandanna work.

He walked down a street off the main, then stood in cover till darkness crept in; then it was a case of waiting for a good citizen to come by. It took a long wait, but then along came a man in smart garb, humming a tune to himself. Rich pulled up the bandanna, moved out smartly so he was behind the victim, and cracked him on the back of the head. The man fell down and Rich searched all pockets. The haul was good. He took thirty dollars and a watch.

He then saw that the man was old and a little on the weak side. It had been an easy attack. So simple, he thought, the business of surviving, as long as you had no scruples. No, scruples had been thrown away, into the wind, a long time back.

Back at the hotel, which stank of sweat and rats, he tried to sleep, and the only thing he could do was let his mind wander into the dream of his future. Rich Seward would walk out of his bar, called out by some jumped-up kid. Out he would walk, padding like a tiger, ruthless and lethal. He looked like some big-name winner, a man the whole territory knew and feared. The kid would see him, shiver at the knees, and run like a jack rabbit.

Yet he couldn't sleep. Something in him took away his peace of mind. Something pulled at him, tugging like a child when it wants attention, wants your time. Only when he was famous would sleep come. Until then he was out to be known, to be a man who walked in a street and people moved aside. Rich Seward, the gunman. Rich Seward, the man you feared. That was all he saw when he closed his eyes.

What he didn't know was that downstairs, the manager and his cronies were already talking about him. He had made them ask questions. Some thought he was there because he was yet another hired man for Rorke. Others suggested that he was one of an endless flow of rogues who came and end up on the end of a rope after a speedy hearing at the miners' court. Nobody recognized him. He was unlikely to be one of the gang that was robbing stages down towards the Gallatin. Rich Seward was becoming a man of mystery, but as yet he knew nothing about that.

THIRTEEN

Bill Davey and Mirez were now riding into Randal, slowly, against the wind. They left the horses and wagon in the nearest stables, and walked to a small bar on the edge of the main street. There was nobody there except the landlord, who was wiping glasses and looking bored. 'Gentlemen, welcome to Randal. What can I get ya?'

'Two beers,' Mirez snapped out and then sat down. 'Bring 'em over.' He put money down on the bat-top.

'I hear there's a trial on some time this week? I come a long way, hoping to catch it.' Bill asked.

'Sure. It's lasted two days already and maybe a day more. It's Declan Rorke who's after the killer of his daughter. Maybe you heard about it up the road. Every traveller passing through gets the story.'

Bill felt a sense of relief. He had worried, all along the tracks, that he might be too late. He was there just in time, it seemed. 'Who is this Rorke, then?' He asked the landlord.

'Oh, he's the richest man for miles around. Nobody knows how he made it so rich. Rumour says he's gone beyond the law, but try to prove it and you're food for worms. He tends to get what he wants.'

Bill Davey knew all about that. He had come with a mission to help the law get it right. The man the landlord described was exactly the Rorke he knew. The Irishman had crushed everybody in his way, back in Illinois. The rumour back there was that he had got rich by protecting businesses. Either they paid up or were destroyed. Bill knew that for sure.

Bill and Mirez drank their beers and listened. The landlord knew a lot. In fact, if Rorke knew how much the man knew, there would be big trouble for him.

'Who's on trial then?' Mirez asked.

'Man called Serlich. I know him. He's no killer, but he's charged with murder. Trouble is, he's charged with killing Rorke's daughter. You see what's gonna happen? Sure as the sun rises tomorrow, Bill Serlich will be jumpin' for Jesus before this week is out!'

Everything was exactly as Bill Davey had heard when news had reached home that Sky needed some help. He was glad that he had recruited Mirez. The job was looking too much for two men.

'This Rorke, he got plenty of guns behind him?' Bill asked.

'Oh, sure. He's got men to call on numbering around a hundred. I tell you, he wants to govern the whole territory. He would be after my little place except it's not worth a bent nickel.'

'Where's the courthouse, friend?' Bill asked, standing up now.

'Just a short walk along here... The Gold Bullet is packed with interested parties too.'

Bill could sense that there was now some urgency in moving into action. They drank their beers and decided to get busy.

*

'So, you're real friendly with my Kate, mister...?'

'Davey. I'm Sky Davey, at your service.' Sky stood up and held out a hand.

The bar was very quiet now. Trouble was expected.

'I wouldn't shake your hand for any lump of gold, Mister Davey...' Cal jerked forward and swung a punch at Sky's chin, but the tall man ducked away and stood ready, fists in front, tight and tough. Cal came at him again, and wrapped his grip around Sky's midriff. They both staggered back, falling over a line of chairs, and the crowd moved back, watching them sprawl on the floor. Cal was first up, and his punch hit home, thumping into Sky's belly. But the big man now grabbed Cal, swung him around so that he was in a grip, and said, 'Now, stop all this or I'll have to hurt you.' He flung Cal forward, hoping for a sign that he had had enough.

But no, Cal ran again, but this time, Davey's fist cracked him right head-on in the face and down he went. Sky sat on him.

Kate came to them now, and told Cal to get up and shut up. But Cal was out cold, and had to be carried into a back room, where Kate fussed over him and talked to him, waiting for him to come round. She was thankful that he had made it home. Nothing else mattered.

The assembled townsfolk stayed well clear of Sky Davey, as he brushed himself off, ordered a whisky, and took his seat by the window. The kid ran in again and said that the trial was resumed.

Harry Wellman crept around, whispering all he could about the dark deeds of the stranger who was now among them, like a bad apple in the barrel.

The kid acting as messenger reported to Harry again and explained that Rorke was not dead, but that a man was arrested for trying to kill the Irishman. 'Heaven help him… who is he?' Dandy asked.

'Joel Borne,' the kid answered.

They all knew Joel Borne. Nobody thought him capable of any crime, let alone violence.

Three old-timers now found the courage to sit around Sky Davey. They took him coffee and some bread and ham.

'Is it true about that time in Denver? The stage robbers? Did you kill all three? I knew one of 'em, you see,' one asked.

Sky went on eating. More questions were fired at him. He said nothing, but only gave them a faint smile. Then one question seemed to hit a nerve. He was asked about the death of his brother, which had been reported with a level of sensation that missed nobody, as it filled all the gossip for months.

'My brother died in the crossfire one time. He was trying to stop a fight. He was a man of peace. I respect men of peace. But you know, the law lets down the common man. It lets him down, and so men like me have to step in. That's why I done what I done.'

Dandy picked up the point, 'Sounds noble, Sky. You make murder noble.'

'No. There's no nobility. It's putting the law straight, pure and simple. It has to be done. Too many men only wear the dark clothes, make the fine speeches, promise plain folk everything, and then do nothing at all to change things. Me – I see that justice is done.'

'Maybe justice is a creature that moves around, slips out of your fingers like an eel?' Dandy asked.

'Well, it might do if you don't act, and act quick. The problem with the law is that it pays a lot of lawyers. They get in the way.'

That time, Sky got a laugh. They were warming to him. On his side, he finished his food and whisky and said that he was there just on his way north.

'You sure you ain't here for no reason connected to that trial, Davey?' Someone asked.

'I'm watching what might happen because it's interesting. There's too much routine. I get restless in routine. Routine means days and days and nothing… just like a great plain stretching out north, the same for a week's riding.'

The old-timers walked away, as they had had enough now, and they saw that there was only limited information to be teased out of the man. Their card game was about to be resumed, when the kid ran in with a new message. 'New juryman sworn in. The man who tried to kill Rorke was on the jury!'

He was right. A new deputy had been sworn in too, and he was sitting watching Joel Borne in the jailhouse. Jack Hamer was more troubled than ever. He knew he had to move quick, back to the court, but his mind was in turmoil. The young man was telling the truth, surely. Hamer paused in the street, saw that he was by the church again, and went in, half of his mind telling him to arrest Teller, Rorke and the lot of them. But where would he find an army?

Padre John was in prayer. But when he heard the door swing shut he stood up and turned around. Jack Hamer's stare was right at the Padre's face. His look searched the priest for some kind of reaction.

102

'I know why you're here, Jack. I expected you back. What's happened?

'What's happened? I'll tell you what... the worm is ready to turn. I need your help.'

Padre John could see the stress and strain on his friend's face.

'Tell me, and make it simple.'

'I'm outnumbered, but I have to do something... something drastic.'

What's the situation?'

'To put it boldly, my old friend, I'm up against the man who runs this place, his lawyers, his gun-men and his dollars, and my job is to save an inno-cent man from the noose. That make sense?'

'Sure. It means I have to pray for you. Maybe you could pray too, or do you think you have the strength down there... down inside you?'

'I'm trying to fool myself into thinking I have, Padre.'

FOURTEEN

The kid running with the messages and reports was being kept busy. He had come to see that if he listened in on every conversation, he would always find something to his advantage. This policy paid off when he saw how interested the old-timers were in the stranger they called Sky. He buzzed around, taking coins from various people who wanted inside information. Everybody knew the kid darted in and out of the courtroom, but now he was darting across the street and watching everything that happened. When he saw the two strangers walk out of the little cantina he followed them to a boarding house where they checked in, and he heard their talk as they sat out on the sidewalk.

Bill was telling Mirez what the plan was for the action, as soon as there was news about the trial ending.

'See, Sam, I'm about to call on Sky. We'll then have a notion of when it's all ending, and when the sheriff walks out with the prisoner. He'll head towards the jail, naturally. Now, when that happens, you'll be watching the back door, as I'll watch the jail side. Sky will take care of the front door. Whatever they do with the prisoner, we'll be there, covering it. See? Now have another beer. Soon as we hear from The Gold Nugget, we split up and take our positions.'

'Understood, Bill. Now take it easy. We had a long ride!'

The kid had all this stored and he knew that more than one person would be interested in the news.

In the courtroom the new juryman had been sworn in and took his place. Raines was doing everything he could now for Serlich, and he was entirely ignorant of what he was up against. The outburst by Joel Borne had made him think, and had cast a dark shadow over everything he was doing to save the neck of his client. What if the young man's accusations were true? But there was no time to dwell on that. Witnesses had been hard to find. Only two people would testify against Rorke, and one of them was at the stand now. This was a man who had been working in the Serlich house the day before the deaths. He was Henry Binns, and he was nervous, to say the least. He looked learned, formal, with glasses and a conservative, formal suit and vest on him.

Raines was dealing with him gently. 'Mr Binns, you live away out from Randal, is that right?'

'Yes sir, about thirty miles away. But Mr Serlich, he needed a carpenter and he knew me from way back, when he worked not far from my place.'

'You were working in the house the day before the deaths, then?'

'I was. I was repairing the staircase and putting in some special rails I'd made, carved with a design that Mrs Serlich asked for.'

'Did you see or hear anything that might have any bearing on Mrs Serlich's relationship with Dan Beech? Because I understand that Mr Serlich was away from home that day?'

'Well yes – yes, sir. It's a delicate matter.'

'Mr Binns, we need to hear these things, despite the fact that they are delicate. You do understand the importance of this? Mr Serlich could lose his life.'

Declan Rorke was not happy. His men had not been able to track down Binns. There had been no chance to bribe him or even to remove him if he refused a bribe.

'Well sir, I did see some *intimacy*.'

There was a sudden burst of amazed and shocked people across the lines of seated public ranks. The man was Raines' best witness. He was having an impact.

'Mr Binns, could you explain what you mean by "intimacy" please?'

'They were in the sitting-room. I think they forgot I was out in the hallway. I could see Mrs Serlich kissing Dan Beech. It was very… very strong. I'm pretty sure they were close… closer than they should have been.'

There was more reaction from the public. The sounds were like the swell of a tide, ebbing and flowing with every comment made, and then with every short silence.

'Mr Binns, would you say that Sarah and Dan were *lovers?*'

Binns actually blushed. He sensed Rorke giving him a hard stare.

'Yes, sir. I would say they were pretty hot for each other. I also heard words spoken.'

More hubbub. This time the noise was like a crowd in a market-place, and Judge Baker had to order silence in court.

'Please go on, Mr Binns.'

'Now, what I mean by that is … well, that I heard Mrs Serlich say something very… er… very affectionate.

'Affectionate. Explain please.'

'She said, *he's not back till tomorrow. We're free to make the most of it.*'

Teller snapped out an objection. Rorke shouted in a rage. Bill Serlich was silent and at the same time, sick at heart.

Judge Baker called for order again.

'Mr Binns, would you say that Dan Beech was, shall we say, forcing or pressuring Mrs Serlich into anything she didn't want to do?'

'Not at all. She was keen for some lovin', if you ask me!' This time he looked across at the audience. He was not so shy any longer. There were some laughs among the shocked responses.

'Thank you, Mr Binns. That is all.'

Teller allowed some time before he stood up to cross-examine Binns. Rorke was whispering at him, goading him to do something.

Teller tried the friendly approach. He walked close to Binns, and gave him a broad smile to put the man at his ease. 'Mr Binns, you are, I understand, a good trustworthy craftsman?'

'Sure.'

'You have how many years of experience working with wood?'

'Twenty or more, I guess.'

'You do some very delicate carving, real close-up work… enough to strain a man's eyes. I see that you wear glasses.'

'There is some wear and tear on the eyes, yes.'

'Wear and tear on the eyes, so your eyesight is impaired. You might not see things so well? Would you agree with that?

'I guess.'

'So we could assume that on that day, when there was supposed intimacy going on, you might have not seen what you thought you saw?'

Binns looked unsettled. He looked around him and seemed uneasy about why he was there and what this examination was all about. 'No, I know what I saw. They were kissing… he was putting his hands in places that a gentleman shouldn't place his hands. I should have said that.'

Teller seized his chance to find further weakness. 'Ah, so you should. Now you're saying things about what you *should* have done. I'd say you were unreliable.'

'Not at all.' Binns was losing his temper.

'Ladies and gentlemen, I suggest that this man heard and saw nothing at all in the Serlich house. I suggest that his testimony is unreliable. Good workman though he may be, his trade has worn him down so that he is unable to function fully. His sight is weak. He should never be on this witness stand. No more questions.'

He sat down. He and Rorke looked smug and content.

There was one more witness for the defence, then it would all be over and the attorneys could sum up and sentence would be passed. Rorke was in a good mood.

*

But over in the jail, the sworn-in deputy was destined to be in big trouble. Young Joel Borne had not taken his capture and locking up too well. In fact, burning in him now was a thought that was taking over his whole being. More than ever before, deep inside he felt an urge to set things right himself, to get back at the lousy lawmen in his town who were dirtying the name of the law. Someone was going to be punished for what they did to him, for how they laughed at him in the jury room.

Joel studied the deputy and saw his weakness. The man was eating. He did nothing else but eat and drink. Joel could see that the man was weak. So he played on his sympathy, acting like a child, as the man was old enough to be his grandpa.

'Say, mister… do you think I could have a slice of that cake? I ain't eaten nothin' since this morning.'

The man looked at him and decided to be kind. He walked across and foolishly put his hand near the bars, as he held out the cake. Borne grabbed the hand, yanked the man to the bars till he held him firm, and then reached for the man's gun. The barrel was sticking into the man's head in seconds. 'Now, hand me the keys… with your free hand. If you don't, I'll blast a hole in your head.'

The deputy did as he was told. Joel swung the door open and then went to the man, who was cowering on the floor, with a hand held high to protect him. It didn't stop Joel's pistol coming down as he pistol-whipped the man, grabbed him and threw him inside the cell.

The key was turned. The deputy was out cold, stretched across the sawdust. Out into the street, gun in hand, went Joel Borne, and he was out for revenge.

FIFTEEN

Rich Seward thought that looking for trouble was better than waiting for it. The man he wanted was somewhere in Randal, and he tried asking around. That brought no response. Nobody seemed to know the name of Sky Davey. That was until he thought of the obvious: a newspaper office. They knew everything, and a bonus was that Rich Seward wanted the papers to know about him.

He found Gotty sitting at his desk, reading through the feature piece on Sky before going into print. Destiny must have had Rich in mind as he walked in that day.

'Say mister, you the newsman?' Rich asked, leaning on a cabinet and looking around the room.

'You're in the right place for that. What can I do for you?' Gotty didn't like to be disturbed.

'Name's Rich Seward. I'm trying to find a local resident, name of Sky Davey. Can you help?'

Gotty laughed, he was so surprised. 'Now Rich Seward, what kind of mystical force is working in you, that you walk in here, asking about the man whose face looks at me from my desk? See… look here!'

Rich walked across, looked at the paper, saw the picture of Sky and asked, 'That him? That Sky Davey?'

'Sure. There it is… his name. See?'

'Ah now, the thing is, mister, I'm not so good with letters and words and such. I missed out on school.'

Gotty leaned back, put his hands behind his head and frowned. 'What do you want with a notorious gunman, young fella?'

'Well now, if I told you, you would have a good story for that there paper. See, I'm asking about the man because I'm plannin' to call him out. You need to be there with your notebook.'

'Call him out? Is this some kind of game? You can't have been reading cheap novels, so how come you're wanting to kill a man?'

'It's easy to answer that mister. I want to be in your paper. *The man who gunned down Sky Davey.* I can see your front page.'

Gotty now saw that he was dealing with an unhinged mind. This character was dangerous. There was only one thing to do – humour him. 'So you're going to take Sky Davey, are you, young man? Well now, what can I write about you? You would sell papers for me, son.'

'What can you write about *me*? Now, where can I start? I got three notches on my grip for a start. I'm an orphan who's fought his way to the top when it comes to gunslingers… I hope you're writin' all this down.'

Gotty took pen and paper and pretended to scribble.

'You're lookin' at the man who faced up to Pueblo Manny. He was so yeller he ran for it… said he was too drunk to fight. In short, you are writin' about the next Sky Davey, only bigger than that jumped-up nobody. You follow me?'

Gotty couldn't believe the puffed-up nonsense the kid spoke. In his trade he had come across a number of similar types. They all read about some supposed lightnin' draw cowpoke who won a shoot-out in a cowtown encounter. Then they took to the road with the man's name imprinted on their minds, hungry for glory. Maybe it was risky, but Gotty decided to put a hole in that nice fancy shirt called glory that the kid wanted to wear.

'Son, listen to me. You have to forget this and go home. I seen so many men eating dirt with a smokin' gun over them and a coffin-maker askin' who's likely to pay the bill for burial. What's it all for? There are a thousand reputations in your line of work, and they blow away on the wind every day of the week. Go home, Rich Seward, go home now.'

Seward's face was reddening up. He did not want to hear any supposed good sense. 'Sir, I respect you for runnin' a paper and such, but I have to ask, what do you know about shootin and such? Another thing… I ain't got no home. Never did. My home, sir, is the open range and the nearest arroyo. My roof tends to be what a cottonwood tree can offer, but mostly the heavens. Now don't preach to me about going home. It's the kinda home I got that makes gunfighters.'

'Fine. If that's the way you see it, then let me know where and when you plan to stand up to Sky Davey, and I'll be there.'

'I have to find the man first.'

Gotty saw his story growing bigger and more compelling with every second that ticked by. Not only could he have a profile of a killer, but he could have that killer facing a little upstart rat, and right here in Randal. He decided to change again and encourage the kid. 'You know what, young Rich Seward, you persuaded me. Sure, now if I could tell you where you can find Sky Davey, you have to make sure I'm there to see you two staring across the road and grabbing guns from your belts. Though let me tell you that the man you're seeking is formidable, boy.'

Rich hated that last word. His fist came down on the desk so that it shook, and Gotty pulled back, out of reach of a punch. 'You don't call me that, mister! Nobody ever calls me a boy. I never was a boy. I had to be a squealing infant and then a man right after. There was no *boyhood*, you hear?'

The newsman was genuinely fearful. He saw then what power there was in the man, and what deep hatred. This kid thought that the world owed him something.

'You got that, right? Because one thing Rich Seward will never do is back down. He'll never back down and go home. Going home is for the cowards, and I met plenty of them!'

Gotty switched now to the man with a story, and it was growing and growing all the time. 'Right, Rich Seward, your name will figure in my paper. If you beat Sky Davey, then you'll be front page. You satisfied with that?'

'Sure. You're in at the beginning, mister newsman. Years from now, they'll be writin' songs about me. Fact is, you could write it now and git in there first. Call it *The Ballad of Rich Seward*. Give it some punch. Be sure to mention this here bull jewel hanging around my neck... it's my lucky charm. Pueblo Indian made it for me.'

Gotty almost burst into laughter. He had met some kids hungry for fame, but never one like this. Seward had self-love in buckets and more confidence than a liquor salesman in a dry saloon. 'Sure, I'm making a note about the bull!' Then he said:

'Well, Rich Seward, you are a five-minute walk away from your man. I'll take you there soon. But first you need to know something. There's a big court case going on, and like to finish in around a half hour, so I'm told. Now, we newsmen like to maximize our material. If you sit and drink a coffee with me now, by the time we drink that and enjoy

some desultory talk, there will be lawmen escortin'
their prisoner out of the court, and Sky Davey will
react. I don't know how, but he's watching that
courthouse like a hog expecting his swill. Okay?'

Rich thought for a minute. He was excited at the
thought of being so close to the man he wanted,
and it went down hard having to wait any longer to
meet him. But the paperman in front of him was
going to make reputations, put him centre page
for sure. 'Let's have that coffee!' he said, sitting
down opposite Gotty, with his legs up on the desk.

SIXTEEN

When Bill Davey walked into the saloon, he did so with his slicker round him and his hat low. He ordered a beer, and then looked around shiftily. He was searching for his son, Sky, and he found him, still at the window seat. He went across nice and easy, and tapped Sky's arm. When his son looked up, his face opened up with delight.

'Pa… you made it! I thought you would miss it… comin' all that way… how did you get here on time?'

'It was chance. I just pushed on, as I heard the trial was coming fairly soon. That man you sent… on the stage. He told me. I was on the road quick as lightnin' after that. Now, let me sit down and let's be real quiet. We're so near, so we can't mess up now, son.'

'We won't.'

'That man, he's got it comin', and his days are numbered.'

They had to cut the chat. Kate came to them. She wanted to put things right between herself and Sky.

117

'Cal… he was out of control. Sorry about that, Sky. He's asleep now. I gave him something to help him rest a while. Trouble with Cal is he's hot-headed.' She then noticed the newcomer.

'This is my father, Bill. Just arrived. We're movin' on tomorrow. Got a job of work in the north. Some miners need a little help.'

Kate noted the armoury on Bill. He had two revolvers and a long knife tucked in a cross-strap.

'I see. Well, my hotel never had such profits. A little trial is so good for business. You should be proud of your son, Mr Davey. He's been a big help to me since he arrived.'

'Oh, he's a useful man to have around… don't believe all the rumours about him.'

When Kate left them to talk, they had a lot to think about. 'Word is, pretty soon now, Hamer's set to walk out, cuffed no doubt to his prisoner. They have to walk maybe five hundred yards to the jail. There'll be a crowd behind them, coming out into the light. When do we take our man, son?' Bill Davey, now enjoying his rest, asked.

'Pa, first thing, there are two doors. There's a back door…'

'Ah, true. Now I should tell you that we have help. I have a man watchin' the back. I met him on the trail… named Mirez. Seems reliable.'

Sky was not too pleased. 'Pa, we said it was our job. What if this Mirez does the work for us? What if we're robbed of the satisfaction?'

'Steady son, steady. What matters is that he dies today, or tomorrow if for any reason the trial goes on. That's all.'

'I guess it'll soon be over. One thing we have to watch, of course. There'll be that crowd. We might gun down some innocent standing around. I know I'm a good shot, but it bothers me, Pa.'

Bill Davey wiped some beer off his chin. 'We can only do our best, son. I have every faith in you. I seen you shootin' cans and boxes, when you were knee high. Guns and weapons have been a part of you since you was out of your mother's arms. I remember you throwin' knives as well. You could have been a soldier-boy!'

'Oh no. Soldierin' is for fools. But okay, we take risks. I'll do my best. Maybe they'll all stand still for the newsmen. They've been hanging around here since I came.'

Bill gave a wry smile. 'I read about you in the papers, many a time. I could hardly tell my friends I was proud of a gunslinger, but inside I knew you was on the side of right. I know that you were not out for blood-money, son. You must have done the killin' for some worthwhile reason.'

'I did it to help folk who had been let down by the law. The law out west, Pa, it's slippery as a fresh-netted eel. One day the marshall might lock up the bad man, but the next day, the marshall breaks the law. I kept meeting people who came to me with a sense of wrong, of injustice. I had to do somethin', and I'm sure you know that. But the press want me to be a ruthless killer.'

'It's the way of the world son, mostly out here, where a man can hang without a proper trial. Once the law steps down from true authority, there's danger everywhere, and even the church folk pray one day and rob the next.'

'Now Pa, I'm not arguing with you there. We know what the man did. We know he's got some vengeance comin' his way. Now you have this man Mirez with us. He's sure to stay at the back, and one of us takes the spot here, with a clear look at the front of the courthouse. The other goes down a-ways, towards the jailhouse. Which is you?'

'Son, I'll take the stretch towards the jail.'

'It's settled. Are you sure this man is reliable?'

'I trust him. It's in his eyes. I can read a man pretty well.'

'Let's hope so, because if the crowd goes out the back, we have to be sure this Mirez goes for the right man.'

'I gave him a picture, from the newspaper. It's a good likeness.'

They were not in the mood to smile. It was too early for any celebration, but they did clink glasses, and when his drink was done, Bill Davey went out into the street to take his position. The word was that it would not be too long before the trial was over.

*

In the courtroom, Jed Raines called his last witness. It was the final throw of the dice. He knew that the whole place was against Bill Sertlich, but at least Rorke had wanted a correct, legitimate trial. It was never a matter for the miners up the road, where a wrongdoer could be dragged off to a room, locked in, asked a few questions, and then dragged to meet his end in a noose. That had happened only a month earlier. Raines was thankful for small mercies.

Over the meal break, he had talked to Serlich and tried to reassure the man, but Serlich was cracking. There were signs he was going to break. His eyes were welling up. He wrung his hands together, and kept putting his head down, as if half in prayer.

'Bill,' Raines had said, 'Bill, listen to me… I've been in this situation before. The West is full of these greedy men, desperate for power, ready to turn every good thing dirty and to sully the good name of a man or a place. Rorke is one of these men. I'll not let him win here. You fired in self-defence. We spoke the truth.'

Serlich had been hard to convince. They both needed a boost from somewhere, and maybe Martha Medd would provide that.

'You Honour, I call my last witness, Martha Medd.'

A middle-aged woman shuffled in, wrapped in several layers of clothes, with a lace shawl around her chest and over her chin. She was prim and formal in everything; her clothes were mostly black and her face was thin, as if her body had been deprived of sustenance and she looked out at the world expecting nothing but pain.

She took a seat, swore on the good book and then looked at Judge Baker, wanting reassurance. He managed a smile, but nobody in that room was convinced by it. The man was miserable as a funeral in winter.

Martha fiddled with her shawl, adjusted herself on the chair, and then looked towards Jed Raines, who stepped a little closer to her and smiled. His smile was more convincing, but it hid desperation and a vain hope that the jury might listen instead of picking their noses and whispering about somebody's new mare or the next stage arrival.

'Mrs Medd, I understand that you are a widow?'

'Yes, sir. I lost my Herbert three years back this November. He was fine one day, all happy and cheery, and then the next day he started coughing. The Good Lord only knows what got in him, but it sent him to his grave two days after the first cough. I tried everything my mother taught me, and she had been a true medicine woman, as she knew all the...'

'Mrs Medd, please… just answer the questions and keep it a little more brief please. Could you do that?'

The people around the court were amused. It was not a good sign for Bill Serlich. Jed wanted serious, he wanted exact, and he wanted a picture in the minds of the jury of a man who had stolen another man's woman.

'Mrs Medd, you worked as a cleaner and cook for the accused, Bill Serlich?'

'Certainly did. I cooked special meals too… Mr Serlich adored my cherry pies…'

This time, Raines cut in, to stop any further digression.

'Now, Mrs Medd, of all people, you would know if there were any signs of a relationship between Sarah Serlich and Dan Beech. Am I right in that assumption?'

'You are right, sir. Many a time I heard whisperings when Mr Beech called in. They ate together. They laughed a lot together.'

'So you would say that the two of them were very close, and Sarah was a married woman?'

'Oh, very close. They was always hugging. Truth is, I was like part of the furniture. They never noticed me. I don't think that Mr Beech ever addressed one word to me, that's the Lord's truth, I swear. It's like I was a stove or a table, for all I counted in that house. Though Mr Serlich was always good to

123

me. You do want me to say good things about Mr Serlich, right? As he's the one in trouble here?'

There was more laughter. Bill Serlich flushed red. Jed Raines felt that she had to go. The woman had left her good sense at home. But he tried one more question.

'Mrs Medd, in your experience, what would be your opinion of Mr Beech?'

'Objection!' screamed out Teller. 'This is irrelevant…'

But Baker genuinely wanted to know about Beech, so he allowed the question. 'No, you carry on, Martha. Tell us about Beech.'

She did. She had very strong opinions about the man. 'Dan Beech was no good, Your Honour. Dan Beech took pleasure in making enemies. He was a lady's man years back when I first knew him. After mining went up the creek he was skint, and he went to the drink and then he turned nasty. I had no time for the man. I could never see what lovely Mrs Serlich saw in him that was so irresistible. He was only interested in one thing… getting her into bed! There, I said it. I told Mr Raines I would come here today and tell you folks what a monster that man was. Well, I said it.'

Bill Serlich's head was in his hands, and he stared down at the wooden floor, despair engulfing him. Raines told Martha Medd that there were no more questions, but then Teller told the judge that he had something to ask. He stood up, walked around a little and finally let the silence work for him, as it unsettled Martha. She was expecting torment and she got it, but it came at her like Satan when he changed into a snake.

'Mrs Medd, do you consider yourself to be an upright citizen of this town? One whose words all good folk should heed and respect?'

'Why of course, everybody in this room knows that me and my husband have always been church-goers, and we have given to every charity. I have worked myself to the bone for this town…'

'Now Mrs Medd, that may all be true, but may I remind you about something four years back in Randal… something about a charge of a whore-house?'

There were whisperings and groans in the court and Mrs Medd clammed up. Then finally she said, 'Are you implying something unsavoury, Mr Teller?'

'You may be sure I am, Martha. Because you ran such a place, I believe?'

She now snapped her answer. She was petulant. 'I did not run a whore house. I owned a theatrical entertainment palace. My girls were dancers from back east, and they were ladies. They all had college diplomas in the Thespian arts!'

Laughter again. Some of the audience thought that anything Thespian was pretty low down. Teller had made his point, but he pushed home mercilessly.

'Mrs Medd, I suggest that anything you say in court today is suspect. How can these good people trust the word of a madame, a keeper of a brothel house, a sporty place for the rougher breed of men?'

Martha blushed and moved about on her chair. Teller released her from her torture. 'No further questions, Your Honour.'

SEVENTEEN

Jack Hamer ran his finger across the tin star on his chest. It was there for a reason, and you didn't wear it lightly. His mind was now in a place where there was a deep shadow over every thought. Something inside him wanted to examine everything he had done since that first visit from Declan Rorke. He sat in church, left to himself, and his mind went back to the time Rorke called into the office. The Irishman had sat at the desk, shaken hands and given his name: 'I'm Declan Rorke. I just bought a mine... oh, and a stage company. I need to be sure the law will take care of my land... everything I own. Can I rely on you?'

A roll of banknotes the size of barrow-wheel was slid across the desk. Jack Hamer saw that roll in his mind now, as he sat in the Lord's house. Back then, he had stared at it, frozen in indecision. Rorke had said, 'Hamer, I hear your wife is real sick. Needs a good medical man. I know such a man, the best in Montana territory. Word is that you like a gamble too... reckon that depletes the family finance, hey?'

The silence had seemed like hours. He stared at the dollars, and Rorke spoke quietly and persuasively. Then Hamer reached out and took the money. Rorke had stood up, shaken hands and left, saying, 'Good to know I can trust the law. Very comforting, Sheriff Hamer.'

Now what had been the consequences of that, Hamer asked himself, sitting there, thinking of all his mistakes. Then he thought of the bottle of whisky in his office and he wanted to walk back and smash the thing.

A man can only take so much. He thought about the times, too many to count, when Rorke had sent a man to leave a command. It was always such things as 'Let the man be at the Silver Stream tonight', or 'Need to have a shipment stopped'. Most times it was that Rorke wanted a man arrested and locked up, or escorted out of town. How much could a man take?

He considered his situation. He was alone now. Truth was, he had nothing to lose. Nothing more dangerous than a man with nothing. He looked around the church. It was bare, empty. There was a simple cross at one end, and rows of plain wooden benches. Nothing glinted or shone anywhere. Padre John lived the simplest of lives. He woke at dawn, worked in a little vegetable patch, ate twice a day, led prayers, gave a weekly service, buried and married and baptised folk.

That's the kind of life I want, Hamer said to himself. *I can make that kind of life.*

He rose, walked across to Padre John and tapped him on the shoulder. 'Padre, your silence is louder than any sermon. Tomorrow, or maybe today, you could bury me, or you could bury some others. Either way, you're diggin' holes for sinners.'

Padre John had no idea what that meant, but he put an arm around Hamer's shoulder and said, 'My friend, I want you to remember that everything will be right, in the end. All we can do is make the right choice.'

'What about the ones who make the wrong choices, Padre?'

'They suffer, but will be healed... when the Judgement Day comes. There is always forgiveness.'

Hamer said nothing, but inside he told himself that you had to forgive yourself, and he couldn't do that. What he needed, hungered for, was vengeance on himself for his backing out when he should have done the right thing.

Jack Hamer walked out into the wind, which was still rattling wood, and made his way towards the courthouse. He was going to dish out some justice. It would be a mite late, but it was still justice.

*

'Your Honour, I just want to say a few last words to the jury before they retire.' Teller was enjoying this. 'I want to point out that the accused burst into his home that fateful night and he took the life of a man who he thought was over-affectionate to his wife. Now, we have no witnesses. But it is perfectly clear that Serlich was a jealous man, an unpredictable man, one who was quick to act and quick to violence. There is only one verdict today that would reflect the correct process of the law. Gentlemen, you must find Bill Serlich guilty of murder. Thank you for your patience.'

Judge Baker nodded at Jed Raines, who was ready to reply.

'Gentlemen of the jury, what have you seen and heard today? You have heard that witnesses have spoken up about Daniel Beech being a man who seduced women, and he did not stop at single women. No, he worked his fateful charms on married women, good wives, who should have been beyond his workings and plans. Mrs Sarah Serlich was basically good, but she had a weakness. Her husband was away from home for long periods. Why? Well, the answer is that he was working hard to make money. He did not want to take money all the time from his father-in-law. He is a proud man. In fact, it is because he is proud that he couldn't take the sight of his wife being corrupted by Daniel Beech. You have heard what actually happened. A husband came home to find his wife in the arms of this seducer, and the seducer drew his gun. Serlich was fast on the draw, and in self-defence he shot the man dead. These are the facts. Your duty is to acquit this man, and let him go back to his very useful and worthwhile life in Randal.'

There was just one thing left to do in that court: Judge Baker had to sum up. He had watched and listened at length. It was now the time of day when the light was fading a little and the storm was still blowing. He wanted to wind things up.

'Now, I have to address this court with some mighty firm words. By that I mean that we must not be fooled by the words of people called by Mr Raines, telling us what a fine man Mr Serlich is and how dishonourable Mr Beech was. No, the facts are simple. A jealous man lost his reason. He saw what was a nightmare happening before him – his wife being taken away from him. He never stopped to ask himself if *he* was at fault, leaving the woman lonely for so many times, no. Instead he pulled his revolver and blasted Dan Beech into eternity, and the same fate awaited his wife. He says that she tried to wrestle the gun away from him. Well, he's a truly weak version of manhood if a woman beats him for the strength of his grip. With this in mind, I have to urge you good men to find the man guilty on this occasion, and to listen to the wisdom of Mr Teller today. Thank you for your patience. You may leave the court and adjourn to the jury room and consider your verdict. Court adjourned!'

Everyone went out, Bill Serlich and Ry Jodey going first and taking up their places in the back room where they sat, with Serlich still cuffed. Raines was allowed to sit with them for a few minutes. He had some comfort to offer. 'Bill, Bill, listen to me…you did well. It's not a certain guilty verdict.'

Bill Serlich felt lost. He felt defeat deep down in him. He thought that if he could snatch a gun, he would put it to his head and save the hangman a task. All he could say was, 'Always tilted to Rorke. Always. What chance did I have?'

'Hold on, Bill, there is hope.' Raines tried his best to offer comfort. 'If they come back soon, it's bad news. If the clock ticks on, we have hope, Bill.' The clock did tick on, but they were not to know that was because the jurymen were in need of whisky and some food. They sat around, feeding their faces, knowing what the chairman was going to say.

Finally, in they trooped, after telling the usher that they had a verdict. The court filled again, slowly. Everyone took their places. The kid who carried all the news stood ready by the main door, eager to dash across the road and shout the result.

Last back was Judge Baker, who commanded all to sit and then asked the chairman if they had reached a verdict. 'How do you find the accused, William Serlich, on the charge of murder?' Baker asked.

The chairman stood up. He waited a few seconds before saying: 'Guilty, Your Honour.'

There was uproar in court. Everybody had a response and said what had been waiting for utterance inside their pent-up hearts. Most were sympathetic to Serlich, but Declan Rorke, shaking hands with Teller, didn't care about that.

The usual words were spoken, accompanying the black cap on Baker's head, and the kid sprinted out of the room and across to the saloon of the Gold Bullet.

'Guilty! Serlich is guilty... he'll hang!' The kid screamed out.

Sky Davey cocked his revolver and moved closer to the open window. The saloon was almost shifting on its foundations, such was the violence of the reactions. Then, as everyone was distracted by the noise and the whooping, Cal Delano woke up, rubbed his eyes and registered where he was. There was just one thought in his head – to kill the stranger. In his mind, he saw only one thing – the face of Sky Davey. He muttered to himself, 'Made me look a fool, eh? Well, Cal Delano never takes that from no man, let alone a drifter with a false smile and a bag full of lies. No sir, there would be revenge on the stinking cur who snaked in from the trail.'

He struggled to his feet, took his Colt from its holster at the bed-post, and walked out into the crowd, heading for the window where his enemy sat. There was still some blurring in his sight, but he was able to walk forwards as nobody was looking around at anything. They were all dancing, shouting, singing or shouting out, 'Rorke wins again!'

He had the light of the window to guide him. The tall man would surely still be there, lying back like some prince. Well, he was the Prince of Darkness, and he was going back to hell.

EIGHTEEN

In the jailhouse, Jack Hamer was fastening on his best belt and guns. He kept them locked away, and hardly ever used them. But now, his mind was fixed. He had a job to do, but it was the biggest task of his life. He had to turn around everything he had done with, and for, Declan Rorke. There was a show of strength needed, one that he had never shown anywhere before. He threw his last bottle of whisky against the wall so that it shattered into pieces; he spun the barrel of his six-guns and blew the dust off them; he took his keys, locked the door, and started walking into the wind towards the courthouse. The rain had eased, but the wind still blew hard.

Standing along the street, waiting for the noise that would tell him the trial had ended, was Joel Borne, with his thoughts fixed on Declan Rorke. If he knocked out the lead wolf in the pack, he reasoned, it would be a remedy. He stood in half-shadow, a hundred yards from Hamer. Then there was Rich Seward, who was with Gotty Wellman, further away but just starting out for the courthouse.

Above them all, as he had found himself a warehouse with a loft open to the street, with a pulley attached, was Bill Davey, and he could see them all. He checked them all in his gaze, one by one, and sensed something big coming on. But he couldn't act; he couldn't tell Sky or Mirez. The frustration built up in him. All he could hope for was the sight of Rorke coming along, in his sights.

The crowd came slowly out of the court. First was the swell of folks pushing out through the main doors, and then smaller numbers, trickling out. Sky was the only gun trained on the entrance, as he watched for the sight of his target. But it was not to be. A bullet darted past his head and lodged in the wall. The saloon went quiet and everyone dived to the floor or ran for cover out the back. Kate shouted out, when she saw Cal: 'For God's sake, Cal, put the gun down!'

He didn't listen to her. He raised his hand again and was about to pull the trigger when Sky responded with a shot to the man's leg, and he went down with a cry of pain. Kate ran to him. Sky saw her take Cal's gun and he knew it was safe to return to his position. But everyone was out. There was no other person walking out of the court. Rorke had either walked out, or he had gone out through the back door. Sky had to run out into the street and towards his Pa. They now had to act together.

Bill Davey was in the loft, still waiting, and Sky couldn't find him. The only right move was to get to the back door, find Mirez and hope that Rorke was there. He was the man they wanted. He was the man who had taken away the woman at the heart of the Davey's world. She was Sky's mother, and she had been the very heart of their lives. Rorke had ruined her with his threats and assaults when she was left at the ranch one time, with only a couple of hands to help her. Then there had been the last, fatal visit, and Rorke had taken her life, mercilessly, as if she counted for no more than a cigar but in the dirt.

It was chaos in the streets of Randal. People had heard the shots at The Gold Bullet. Now folk were running for cover in the streets. The wind made more noise than the crowds, whipped up louder than before.

Finally, Bill saw Sky and shouted for him to get around the back, where he would join him. They saw Mirez, still in his position, standing and waiting. He said that nobody had come out of the back.

'Damn… it's all down to the crazy sweetheart of Kate over at The Gold Bullet!' Sky said.

Mirez stayed where he was, and the Daveys moved as quick as possible back to the other side of the building. It was fate or providence or call it what you like, thought Sky, because as they turned the corner, there was a scene in front of them that made them freeze in their tracks. In the middle of the street stood Jack Hamer, both hands hovering over his guns, staring hard at a line of men: Ry, the deputy, cuffed to Bill Serlich, Rorke, Teller, and the jury chairman, who was Rorke's right-hand man and his best shooter.

The line of men froze, confronted by Hamer, who fixed his look on Rorke.

'Rorke, you heard of the worm turning? Well, this is the time,' Hamer said. 'I want you to walk over to me, Ry, with your prisoner, real slow, and stand by me.'

'What you fixin' to do, Hamer?' Rorke asked, 'The law has made a decision. This man is to hang in two days' time. That's by order of the court.'

'I'm ignoring you, Rorke, like I should have done years back. The days of you pushing the law around are through. Now bring the man over here, Ry.'

Ry took a few tentative steps, glancing at Rorke and the gunman next to him, who was looking mighty edgy.

'It's fine, Ry. You're my deputy. There's law around here now. From today, we're starting again, and we're doin' everything by the book. Justice is comin' back right now.'

There was a tense moment as Ry reached the half-way point between Rorke and Hamer. Every speaker had to raise his voice over the wind. Now Rorke said: 'One more step and Phil here will put a hole through you, deputy Jodey. You wanna die today?'

Hamer spoke loud but slow. 'Ry, you know me. You know I'll take care of you. Now take a few more steps and join me here.'

There was a crowd gathering. From The Gold Bullet, everybody could see what was happening; back along the street, Rich Seward and Gotty had stopped, and they were joined by a crowd of good citizens who saw a piece of high drama in their main street. There was an ominous silence. Except for the wind howling.

Then Ry tugged at the handcuffs and urged Serlich to move. Both men took a few steps, and Phil drew his gun. As he fired at Ry, Hamer drew and hit Phil straight in the chest. He fell down dead, lying in the dirt. His shot had winged Ry in the arm and he fell, dragging Serlich with him. In the confusion, Declan Rorke pulled his Colt from its holster and pointed it at Hamer.

'Now, Sheriff, mister hero. You were saying about the law?' Rorke laughed to himself. Nobody else found the situation amusing. Ry was clutching his wound and he was bleeding so much that Serlich took the key and freed their cuffs, as Ry told him where the key was. Then Serlich pressed a bandanna on the wound. 'Rorke, admit you've lost and let the Sheriff do what he wants.' Serlich said this with a tone of resignation. He expected more trouble though.

'He can bleed to death for all I care, and you, Serlich, well, I'm aimin' to be the law now. You'll never reach the noose because you're dying right where you lie!' He lifted his arm and pointed the gun at Serlich. There was a crack from somewhere behind, and Rorke's arm was hit hard by something that sent him down in pain, dropping his gun. With a scream of agony he went down, and Hamer had him in a hold, with cuffs ready to use.

Hamer moved quickly to help Ry and take his deputy and his prisoner to the jailhouse. The Daveys helped, and the crowd gave some applause. All eyes turned to Sky Davey, who had fired the shot; he now came forwards and said, 'You got room for me in that jailhouse? I shot Rorke. He was a disease infecting this entire town. I could have cut him out, but I think he should have a trial and get a taste of some justice!'

It looked as though matters were settled, but that was until a voice rang out from the street leading off to the west. It was Joel Borne, and he walked out to where there was better light but more wind. The weather was tearing into everybody, but as Joel was wearing his smartest suit, and not much for warmth, he was almost swaying as he stood there, holding a rifle. He pointed it at Rorke.

'Sheriff, all I want is justice. This man has been acting as though he were the law. I've seen things in that courthouse that should fill every good citizen with shame. This man, Sheriff Hamer, bribed every legal professional today. I saw it with my own eyes… money passed hands, was slyly tucked into pockets, and the best work of the attorneys in there would never save the neck of this man. Thank the Good Lord that you did something. But the truth is evident. Rorke must die, and I'm going to see him to hell!'

'No, son, this is not the way!' Hamer took a step towards the gunman. 'This is not the way, because if you kill this man, *you* will be breaking the law. You must see that, Joel?'

Joel lowered the barrel slightly. Hamer pressed home his advantage, walking closer to the man, and saying, 'Joel, I knew your big brother Simon. He would be proud of you for saying what you just said... but he would hate you, despise you, for becoming a murderer in your present state of mind. Put the gun down, son.'

Joel felt his heart thumping in his throat. Part of him knew that the lawman was talking sense. But still another part of him was feeling the sheer exhilaration of being the man with the power of life and death over the ruthless liar and fraud who sat on the ground, bleeding.

Hamer could wait no longer. He played his ace. 'Joel, I knew your brother. He's in San Francisco, and he'll read the paper. He'll read about his kid brother who did the civilized thing, not the kid brother who was worse than the man he killed. Right? Think of that.'

Joel did think of that. He lowered the rifle, and Hamer took it from him.

It was tough for Sky and Bill Davey. All that long night they were to talk about how they had not seen things through. They came to Randal to kill the man, and they applied some mercy instead. Now Rorke would sweat it out in the jail.

'You saved a man's life, Sky. We all saw you shoot to save the life of my deputy. Right folks?' He appealed to the crowd, and they all agreed.

It was a full jailhouse that night. The Daveys stayed to be there in case any of Rorke's associates turned up looking for trouble. Serlich was locked up, but Joel Borne gave a full account of what he had seen and heard in the trial.

Hamer took control.

'There will be a new trial, Mr Serlich. You've been through hell. Why, not long back you were thinkin' about your neck bein' stretched. Now you're havin' a fair trial. I'll see to that. Mr Jed Raines will be having a call from myself and my deputy here and we're locking him up… unless he's shifted himself out by now!'

The Wellmans were writing up a new and different story, and they called in to see Hamer, too. There was Rorke, after everyone had gone, leaving Hamer and Ry to get back to normal. There he was, lying on a bed behind bars, after the doctor had patched up his arm. The Wellmans wanted to fire questions at him. Gotty asked, 'What's he charged with, Jack?'

'He's charged with corruption, bribery, robbery, and accessory to murder. I reckon we got four deaths chargeable to him.'

Gotty wrote everything down while Harry asked more questions. Then at last Hamer threw them out and settled down to guarding his prisoners and making sure that Declan Rorke stayed well enough to go to his trial.

'Jack Hamer, you're a prize fool,' Rorke said, 'You can't win. I got plenty more lawyers and lots of dollars to see I come out of the court fresh and clean. Nothing you have is gonna stick. I got an army of helpers. What you got? A deputy and maybe these two drifters from Denver who came here lookin' for me. I know them. They once had a pretty woman to love... no more though. Life is so cruel, don't you think? My arm will heal. Their hearts will carry on festering!'

'Shut your mouth, Rorke. Your days are numbered.'

Nothing gave Hamer and Jodey greater pleasure than sitting and reading newspapers while their prisoner sat there, with his wound throbbing after the bullet had been prised out. As for Bill Serlich in the next cell, he was happy just to throw in the occasional word, such as, 'Rorke, I'll see you hang!'

As the night came on, Rorke could find no sleep. His pain was too intense. There was no drink to help, and not a drop of sympathy from his captors.

Over in The Gold Bullet, Bill and Sky Davey persuaded Kate to let them talk to Cal, who now found
it in himself to apologise. He confessed to having an anger problem. He said he tended to get
moody and had lost control. He was forgiven, and
Kate made the right kind of atmosphere for a night
of celebration when she gave out free drinks and
brought out her girls for the birthday celebration.
'They've been working hard, Cal, for you... Now,
everybody!' She announced from her stage, 'Let
me present to you, The Gold Bullet Troupe, and
their presentation of *A Night in Vienna*... girls!'

The miners, carters, shopkeepers and general
drifters in the now burgeoning and confident territory of Montana, sat along in their chairs, downed
plenty of beer and whisky, and gave the desired
volume of applause as the dancers treated them to
some bare legs and lifted skirts. Then, come eleven
or so, the girls mingled, with Kate, and everyone
danced.

The entire evening gave the town a feeling of
being free of that relentless process of law, with a
man jailed and destined to die, in the grip of a man
who saw himself as all but a king. Now he was a
prisoner, and he was in great pain. That was cause
for celebration.

Sky was disappointed. The plans had not
worked out. Bill Davey was even more so, as he

had journeyed over a vast distance, chancing every-thing, not even knowing if he would get to Randal in time to help. Yet at least the man they hated and reviled was safely locked up.

The future seemed bright. Hamer sat back, around midnight, and stroked that tin star. Now he felt it belonged on his shirt. He had no idea that trouble still haunted the darkness outside. Though Sky would go to his bed tired but content, he was ignorant of the man out in the dark, itching to call him out for a fight. Rich Seward still saw himself in the newspaper headlines, and if he could beat the man who shot Declan Rorke, so much the better.

NINETEEN

He kept out of the light. He was going to give it
one more night in the shadows. Back he went to the
boarding-house, and to whisky and a meagre supper. The fight could wait a little. He sat and brooded
on how the day had robbed him of a plain chance
to face the man. There had been so much going on
that his own plans had been sidelined. The small
town was liable to attract big trouble, he thought.
There had been mayhem in the main street, and
it had looked like every loose and wayward man
around Randal had turned up for some action.

The row and the general hubbub of the crowds
had spoiled what should have been Rich Seward's
day. Yet, still, he reflected, he had been given more
time to weight matters up and dwell a while longer
on Sky Davey. Rich had seen and heard everything,
from his place in the front line of the townsfolk
who had pushed closest to the street battle when
Rorke had walked out with the condemned man.

He had latched on to the fact that Davey now
had another man with him – his own father. Maybe

he could take care of both men? He was confident in that. The father was too long in the tooth to be any sort of problem.

Still, there was one minor piece of preparation to see to. After eating, he walked out in the dark, kept to the shadows, and delivered his note. It said simply, '*Wait at The Gold Bullet, nine tomorrow. You'll have your big story.*'

Then he needed something to stave off the boredom. Rich had to be doing something, and right now he needed some female company. He knew where the whores plied their trade. The cash in his pocket, profit from his robbery, would be enough for plenty of entertainment down there. He went down to the place the landlord had pointed out, and sure enough, there were lights shining bright along a line of maybe six bars, and a barrel organ was playing. Men walked around in the street, some already unsteady on their feet from too much liquor.

The place was everything you would expect from such a low-down dumping ground of humanity. There were screams and cries in the streets. Two drunks tried to slug out a disagreement. Then there, on the sidewalk by the largest building, was a lady of the night, and she was looking for customers, with her madame by her side. They had seen him coming.

'Mister, you looking for company? Come on in!'

Rich Seward could not resist compliments. The madame stroked and fed his vanity, having him sit down in a corner with a young woman on his knee. 'This is Marie. She's out to please you if you got ten bucks.'

He had plenty more than ten bucks, and after buying a bottle of whisky, he took Marie upstairs. She was the last to take her room. The other four rooms were occupied. Some miners had struck lucky and they had cash to spend.

Rich made sure the girl shared his whisky, and he set his hands to work, exploring the girl's body, but when she pulled back and said he was too rough, he threw her over to the wall and she hit her head hard. She screamed out.

Rich was fuzzy in the head when the two men came in. He had left his guns with the madame downstairs, as that was a rule of the house, and these two brick-heads, he saw, carried pistols. They were jabbing the guns forward and comparing his behaviour to that of a coyote or worse still, a rat-tler. That was not a wise thing to do around Rich Seward. 'Do you know who I am?' He snapped out, rage growing in him so that something was going to durst.

'Sure, you're a jumped-up nobody and you're rough with our young lady. Now get out.' The speaker had barely finished speaking when a knife ripped into his throat. Rich had pulled it from its leather belt wrapped around his chest. The man fell back, gurgling and struggling for breath. The other man fired at Rich, but he had ducked and now lunged for the man's legs, dragged him to the ground, as Marie ran out, yelling for help. Rich took the man's gun and pistol-whipped him so that blood ran from a crack in his skull.

Rich Seward sprinted out of there like a jack rabbit hunted by a wolf. He made for the dark, hid himself in a stables entrance, and watched what happened.

Nobody called for any lawman. But he heard someone say, 'Matt's dead, and Bony Robson needs a surgeon real quick.' Someone else asked, 'Who was that damned demon that came to call?'

Predictably, along came Gotty Wellman, and he asked for a description of the killer. It was a hint for Rich to get out of there and find a hole to hide in. The sheriff might search the entire town.

Sure enough, Marie gave a good description to Gotty. When she mentioned a pendant around the man's neck, showing a bull's head, Gotty recalled that from his talk with Rich. He knew who the wanted man was. Then there was the note through the door. There was no doubt who the unwanted visitor was.

It was now late at night. Gotty could see that the man whom the law needed to track down would have run for it. It wasn't worth telling Jack Hamer at that time. It could wait. Gotty was still thinking about Rich telling him what the plans were at The Gold Bullet. He decided to wait till breakfast and sun-up, and then sound the alarm. But that was not what the madame wanted. No, she insisted on bringing in the sheriff. Gotty tried to talk her out of it, but she insisted on being taken to the jailhouse, and she arrived there just as Jack Hamer was locking up for the night.

'Sheriff, I want a man found… a killer! You got a killer in your town. Get busy now and you'll maybe grab him!'

Hamer had the whole story, backed up by Gotty, who gave the killer's name. 'I wanted to leave it, Jack, but this lady has had one of her men shot down dead tonight.'

Jack Hamer had thought that peace reigned in Randal again. He had talked himself into believing that after facing up to Rorke, and making a stand, all would be well. Now here was another murder. And as he replied to the madame he realized there was a gang of men, all armed with rifles and looking mighty angry, standing behind her.

'He's in this town, Hamer. We'll find him, and then we'll try him. He's going to hang. Just thought we'd let you know!' This was Scotch Jamie, who tended to lead the miners and who acted as judge in their court. This was exactly what Jack had been fearing would happen one day – their law would come up against his law.

He could not stop them. He was outnumbered, and he had Rorke to guard. What could he and Ry do against a small army? Once again, he and his law were in trouble, backs to the wall, out west where the books were thrown out every day.

The miners set to work, and street by street they burst into property, shoved folk aside, and searched every room and every corner. They split, and half took the low end of town, while the other half started at the richer side, though they expected trouble. And they got that trouble when they reached The Gold Nugget. It was still full and busy. The music was playing and dancing was still in progress.

When the miners reached the door, there were three men, all Kate's workers, standing in their way. There were threats and curses, and that was enough to bring over Sky and Bill, away from their drinking, to help. Sky went to the front of the ranks standing across the doorway. He fixed his look on Scotch Jamie, who was strikingly similar to a grizzly, all tick hair and layers of deep fat. His chins shook as he spoke. 'We're lookin' for a murderin' pig goes by the name of Seward. We need to search the place.'

Kate was now joining the confrontation, and she replied with, 'No mister, you'll turn away and go home. I don't want any of you people in my hotel.'

'Hotel you call it? I'd say a whore-house, lady!' Scotch Jamie made a huge mistake when he said those words. Sky's fist slammed him hard in the belly, and as he dipped forward, clutching at the pain, the other fist cracked his chin. The big man winced and then let out a whine of pain. Sky put a knee in the man's face, and then, when Jamie staggered back, rolling into his friends, Sky said, 'Any of you men want more of the same, just keep on walking at me!'

Nobody made a move. Bill had his rifle sticking out at them, and now Mirez had turned up and done the same. The miners skulked away.

Kate had plenty of thanks to say, and Sky was only too pleased to help – but who was the man they wanted?

'It doesn't matter,' Kate said, 'I don't care if they were looking for the lowest bounty hunter scum… they're not coming into The Gold Bullet, they are lawless, brutal men who have their own law, and you know what? That is not the future. One day soon, Montana will be run by men like Jack Hamer… and you, Sky… I only wish you could wear a badge and help him out!'

'Couldn't do it, Kate… I need to breeze around. I got a loco weed in my saddle, I guess. I get bored so easy.' Bill Davey nodded and agreed.

Rich Seward was out of town, in a hole. He had found some kind of ditch that a wild critter had pawed out, and safe in that, anybody pursuing him would have ridden past. He dug in, hungry and thirsty and cold. But he had his resolve as strong as ever. He was going to face Sky Davey the next day. In the middle of the night he asked himself, as he

152

had done so many times, why did he bring trouble on himself? It was a question to which he had no answer, and never would.

It was a long night, and he pulled his slicker over him. He had grabbed everything he owned at the boarding house and paid what was due, then hurried out like a hunted deer. Yet still he took comfort in the thought that his appearance would be a shock to the man he was out to get. Even in the worst of situations, there was always the comfort of dreaming about the days that would come, the days when every ordinary Joe west of Kansas would know the name of Rich Seward.

Sleep was a stranger, though. His mind would not, and could not rest. Every strange sound out there made him shiver with shock. He imagined every sound, every breaking branch, to be a bear or a wolf or some beast that was hungry and chasing supper.

His Colt never left his right hand. That gun, he thought, looking at it, with its special decoration of leaves and roses, was his hallmark. That gun would be the gun that shot down Sky Davey.

TWENTY

Sky and Bill had earned that breakfast, and Kate made sure that they had everything they wanted. Mirez joined in, and also Cal, who had mellowed now; the talk was all of the trouble the night before, and Kate had plenty to say. 'The trouble is, Sky, we need more lawmen. Either that or the army. This town is two towns, split right down the middle. Up the north end, there's nobody to stop the worst offences, every day of the week. When a man strikes it rich, or even finds a moderate amount, if he has no strength behind him, and no numbers backing him up, he's doomed. Nobody fights his corner. In steps Scotch Jamie and a dozen more like him. Jack does his best, but he can only watch one place at a time.'

'I'm working on it, too,' Cal put it. 'That's what I've been doing for a while now… looking for companies and concerns that will settle her and bring with them their own staff, their own security maybe. Time's comin' when every rich man, every lucky miner, will want to pay his own lawmen.'

The Daveys listened and learned. Mirez gave his opinion, 'Folks, I would put on a tin star… I'd like to be the third lawman in Randal Course, I'll have to keep on selling things in my spare time, like the cats. Them cats made me three hundred bucks.'

They were all pleased, and some patted him on the back. There was a good feeling all around. When Bill brought up the subject of Declan Rorke, Kate gave the immediate reply: 'That man will stand trial… thanks to Jack Hamer. I knew one day he would stand firm, dig in his heels… it's been coming. I've seen him grow and change…can the job change to match him now? What I want to ask is, how can we get the other crooks? I mean Baker, for one… how many attorneys and men in dark suits were in Rorke's pay?'

As she said this, Gotty and Harry Wellman came in and stood by the bar. Gotty said, 'Well folks, you thought it was all put right, all settled and peaceful. Unfortunately I got bad news. A young man came to see me the other night… he's looking to be a big name.'

'Is that so? Well, he should join a circus or a musical outfit maybe!' Bill Davey joked.

'I'm afraid he's looking for you, Sky. If you look out of the window now, he'll be standing there.'

Sky crossed to the window, to the seat he had got to know very well. Looking out, he saw Rich Seward, in the street, looking up at him. When he saw Sky he yelled, 'Come on out, Davey. It's your day to die!

I'm younger and quicker than you... and you're still full of booze. Come here and face me!'

Sky walked back to his seat, wiped his mouth and looked at the Wellmans. 'I see, you're here for a story. You're here because there's gonna be a casket with either me or that little dog in it! Now ain't you in a noble profession! Pa, if I'm in that casket, make sure there's another going with me, and with a newsman in it!'

He said no more, but went outside, took his place by the sidewalk, looking straight at the challenger, and showed nothing but a firm, serious face and two hands ready to drop to grasp his Colts.

'Ah, Sky Davey... big man, I hear! Well, you've had your turn now and Rich Seward is destined to be the next big name. I hear you're fast on the draw, old-timer. Now, there's always a man faster still, and you're lookin' at him! You've had your day. Now stand aside. You can run away if you like. No dishonour...The newspaper men are ready with their pens.'

'I don't usually face kids. How many years you got... fifteen?'

'It ain't years, Davey, it's skill. I been shootin' revolvers and rifles, and throwin' knives, since the day I first skipped around a back yard. But you, you're long in the tooth I reckon. Move whenever you like.'

So the kid knew the mind tricks, the teasing, the insults that brought up some rage, made a little shake in the arms. He knew all that. Sky knew more, though. Sky had met so many young pretenders. They were predictable, and always irritating, like flies around a steer's head.

Upstairs, Kate was watching, and something in her wanted it stopped. She broke free of Cal, who had a protective arm around her, and she raced downstairs and outside. She went out in the early sun and stood between the two men. This barbarity, she thought, had to stop, and she was going to make it stop.

'Ah damn you, woman!' said Rich, 'You're ruining my big day! Git out of it!'

'Yes, Kate… get back inside, I beg you…' Sky pleaded. 'Leave this to me, Kate, please!'

'No. I want no more street fights. This town has taken too much. There has to be a stop to all this…'

Word was spreading now. With an early start, Rich thought he could do the kill and run out of the place real quick. Now, time was dragging on, and someone called for Jack Hamer. But now the word had brought watchers from all corners of the place. People left their breakfasts and their chores to go and watch. It had been a regular entertainment in Randal, seeing men die in the street, but nobody was bored of it. It still attracted attention, like a travelling show or a phony doctor with a miracle cure. First it was whispers and quiet announcements, then it was yells and excited cries, calling to everyone to drop what they were doing and get out into the main street.

'Lady, I'm countin' to ten and then I'm liftin' my guns… I'm not troubled by puttin' lead through a woman, if I get Sky Davey as well. Now I'm startin' to count…'

Jack Hamer now knew. He was running to the scene with all the strength he could muster, but he was not fast. Just as he reached the point where he could see Rich Seward's back, he heard the counting. He made one last rush, bawling out, loud as possible, 'Kate… fall down… fall down! It's me talking! Jack…'

Rich reached the number ten just as Kate threw herself to the earth. In that split second, Jack reached the scene and he lunged to her side, shielding her. But at the same instant, Sky Davey had snatched both his Colts up and fired rapidly at his man.

There was a cry of pain and Rich Seward doubled over, curling on the ground in a ball of dying agony.

The crowd rushed out to see Jack Hamer on the ground, alongside Kate. Then Sky, holding his shoulder, dropped to his knees. Voices kept asking if anybody was dead, and who had done the shooting. Most of all, who was the young stranger?

After what seemed like hours, with Kate's hand holding Jack's as they both lay flat, the sheriff moved, rolling his body around on its side. Kate struggled to move and then Cal came and helped her to her feet. 'She ain't hit! She ain't hit!' he shouted.

Jack Hamer had been hit in the leg and he was taken to the doctor. Kate was with him all the way, holding his hand, and even kissing his forehead. 'It's a chaste kiss' she said, 'I save them up for you!' Sky was nicked along the side of a knee-cap. Bill and Mirez took care of him. There was nobody to help Rich Seward, but Gotty Wellman stood over the body, taking notes. Rich made the paper all right, but the story belonged to Sky and to Hamer.

A week later, Sky and Bill Davey rode out to go south to the Gallatin valley and spend some time with old friends. Kate and Jack Hamer had tried to persuade Sky to join the lawmen, and take on the miners. But as he said as he rode out, 'I need another horizon, folks. The biggest, furthest possible!'

The Daveys were leaving a new town, a more hopeful town, with a strong sheriff running things. In weeks, Declan Rorke was tried, along with Judge Baker and two more lawyers. The charges were fraud and intimidation, along with bribery and plenty of associated involvement in murder. The Irishman had a good attorney and his neck was saved. His destiny was a very long spell in a very large prison, with guards and high walls.

Bill Serlich left Randal. The rumour was that he made a name for himself way back east in Iowa and then Galena. It seems that lead was still making profits, and he always had a nose for profits. It had lost him his wife, and he was never known to forget talking about her. His trial was in his nightmares, but deep down he knew that he had done no wrong. Sometimes folk pointed at him and said his name. He would always be linked to Declan Rorke, the man who wanted to buy a town and almost did. A man like Rorke always left a stain, along with the pain and suffering that was always in his wake.

As for Jack Hamer, soon he was back to calling in on Kate for a chat and an update on things, and he still went to the church and asked Padre John for advice – but by the end of that year he had four deputies, and the miners stayed clear of him.

Riding into Virginia City soon after, Sky picked up a newspaper and there he saw his face looking back at him, along with Jack Hamer's. It was the story of the 'Six-Gun Vengeance' in Randal, Montana territory. The name Rich Seward was in very small lettering, somewhere near the end of the fourth column of print.